WITHDRAWN

D1521473

THE CORNWELL BRIDE

THE CORNWELL BRIDE

Sheila Walsh

This title first published in Great Britain 1997 by
SEVERN HOUSE PUBLISHERS LTD of
9–15 High Street, Sutton, Surrey SM1 1DF.
This title first appeared in the USA only
in paperback format under the title *The Perfect Bride*.
This first hardcover edition published in the USA 1997 by
SEVERN HOUSE PUBLISHERS INC. of
595 Madison Avenue, New York, NY 10022,
by arrangement with Signet, an imprint of
Dutton Signet, a division of Penguin Books USA Inc.

British Library Cataloguing in Publication Data

Walsh, Sheila, 1928–
  Cornwell bride
  1. English fiction – 20th century
  I. Title
  823.9'14 [F]

  ISBN 0-7278-5164-0

Typeset by Palimpsest Book Production Limited,
Polmont, Stirlingshire, Scotland.
Printed and bound in Great Britain by
Hartnolls Ltd, Bodmin, Cornwall.

Chapter One

The country was still celebrating the glorious victory over Napoleon at Waterloo when the letter arrived at Mountford Grange, a modest manor house on the outskirts of Mountford itself, and with remarkable speed the news spread through the village that Colonel Fairburn had been killed in action.

More than twenty-one years of marriage to a soldier involving long periods of separation had done nothing to prepare Mrs. Fairburn for this moment. As pretty seventeen-year-old Amelia Wallace, she had been swept off her feet by the dashing young ensign, Elliott Fairburn, whose curling locks had gleamed like ripe wheat in sunshine, and whose blue eyes smiled only for her. And despite the intervening years and six children—each one a memento of their brief periods together over the years—that remained her abiding image of him. It was an image in which death had no part, although she had long ago accepted that the army would always come first with him.

For several days Mrs. Fairburn lay in a darkened room, succumbing totally to the ravages of grief, while her maid, Parkin, bathed her head with lavender water and every so often tempted her with a dish of tea, or a few spoonsful of restorative jelly. Even as the days ran into weeks, her recovery was slow.

The Fairburns were well liked in the village, and many neighbors called to offer their condolences. They were received on her mother's behalf by Serena, the eldest of the Fairburn girls, who, at eighteen, was well used to such responsibility, her mother's constitution being far from robust. It was she who presently held the family together with a happy blend of common sense and good humor, while secretly longing for the moment when the door knocker would be still.

She had just closed the door behind the two Misses Treadgolds, who had called with a basket of early peaches from their conservatory, when Edward came to pull at her sleeve.

"Do you know how Papa died?" he demanded with the goulish inquisitiveness of a nine-year-old boy.

"No, Edward, I do not." Serena's voice was unexpectedly sharp. "And I hope you will not ask anyone else such an unfeeling question—especially Mama."

"It isn't unfeeling," he persisted. "In fact, it's very *feeling,* 'cos I wanted to draw a picture of him for Mama, as a valiant hero, which was what the duke called him when he wrote to her."

Serena looked down into the earnest young face, instantly regretting her outburst. She gave him a quick hug. "That is a fine idea, Teddy, but I think, you know, that such a picture might rather upset Mama just now. Why don't you draw her something happy instead—a nice big sunflower, like the one at the bottom of the garden, beside the gazebo?"

"Well . . . if you think that's what she'd prefer." Edward was clearly not convinced.

"I do," she said firmly. "And when you give it to her, pray do not mention Papa."

He scampered away upstairs. Grown-ups were very

strange, he decided, his own head still full of battles. When he was grown up he was going to be a soldier like Connaught and Papa. The memory of Papa's last visit was already a blur in his mind—of a splendid uniform, bristling side-whiskers and a jolly laugh, and a pair of strong arms that lifted him high.

Serena followed him more slowly, her mind once more on practical matters—matters that should not concern her, except that if she did not resolve them quickly, the whole family might suffer. Not for one moment did it occur to her to feel resentful of such a responsibility.

She was, at first glance, a tall, plain young woman who seemed rather older than her years. Her height was accentuated by the current fashion for narrow, high-waisted gowns, and she wore her rich brown hair, her one vanity, brushed until it shone and drawn up into a knot, with a few softening side curls clustered about a pleasant face that could lay no real claim to beauty.

But when she smiled, one forgot that the nose was a little too large, the brow too deep, or that the firm line of jaw hinted at a certain degree of stubbornness and noticed only that her generous mouth curved up at the corners when she smiled, which was often, and that her eyes, more violet than gray, sparkled with merriment.

There was no sparkle in evidence however as, upon reaching the first landing, she looked into her mother's room, where the sound of gentle snoring confirmed that Mama was fast asleep, though later she would roundly deny that she had so much as closed her eyes.

Parkin rose from her chair and hobbled across the room as fast as her rheumatics would allow to assure Serene that all was well.

"She's coming round by degrees, though her constitution

isn't what it was. Keeps on about how she must be down to receive Mr. Price when he comes on Thursday."

"Oh, dear." Serena sighed. "I wish she will not."

The elderly maid shook her head. "Well, we'll have to see."

Serena was still frowning when another short pair of stairs led her to the old nursery, where she found the rest of the family gathered as was usual most mornings. It had become over the years a comfortable and much favored retreat for all, presided over by Miss Abbott, who had come to Mountford Grange as her governess when she was only four—the age Mary was now. Emily had been two at that time, and Harry a mere babe in arms. It had always been a happy place, she thought, watching little Mary struggling valiantly with her letters at the big center table as she herself had once done, and Edward with his tongue caught between his teeth as he concentrated on his drawing. Only Harry was missing. He was away at Eton, though whether it would be possible for him to continue there remained to be seen.

Miss Abbott looked shrewdly at her over her spectacles. "Is everything all right? You are looking tired," she said. "I daresay you have not stopped since breakfast time."

Serena smiled a trifle wanly at the reproving tone of Abby's voice. "It is a busy time. I was beginning to think that Miss May and Miss Aurelia would never leave."

She glanced at her younger sister, sitting near the window, bathed in a shaft of sunlight. Emily was unquestionably the beauty of the family, even in black—especially in black, she conceded without rancor—for it accentuated the creamy perfection of her heart-shaped face and lent added brilliance to the enormous blue eyes and golden curls she had inherited from Papa.

"I had hoped, Emily, that you would come down to help me entertain our visitors."

"Lud, no!" Her sister glanced up from the black lace cap she was stitching for Mama, a look of disdain momentarily marring her lovely features. "The Misses Treadgolds are so odd, I daresay I should have dissolved in a fit of the giggles to see how they sighed over us, and only think how that would have shocked them."

"Miss Aurelia has a big brown bump on her nose." Mary looked up from her labors, chuckling at the thought, and was reproved by Miss Abbott, who told her that it was most indelicate to make comment on the personal appearance of others, and that in any case—and here she cast a reproachful glance at Emily—it was not looks that were important, but kindness.

Emily tossed her head, but the governess was pleased to note that an embarrassed flush stained the exquisite curve of cheek. Sixteen was an awkward age—not quite a child, but not yet a woman. She hoped that discretion might yet come with maturity, but feared that Emily would not improve appreciably with age. Her gaze softened as it passed on to Serena, who had, perforce, grown up too quickly.

"Do come and sit down for five minutes, now you are here. If anyone else calls, I shall instruct Ruby to inform them that you are out."

Serena settled gratefully into a chair near the window, smiling at the notion of Miss Abbott, who had so often exhorted her to tell the truth and shame the devil, resorting to deceit in her behalf.

"There are so many papers to be sorted through before Mr. Price comes," she said with a sigh, "and I must try and get them into some kind of order. I have put him off twice already and cannot do so again. Mother vows she will come down to receive him, but . . ."

"You would leifer she did not?"

"I fear what he has to say might upset her. You know

how flustered she gets. Mr. Price senior would have understood, but his son may not be so discerning."

Not wishing to seem critical of her mother in front of the
younger ones, Serena refrained from adding that in any
case, Mama had not the least idea of managing household
bills. She had already found a number of discreetly worded
demands from local tradesmen, which had been pushed
willy-nilly into a drawer, and had so far been unable to
trace any evidence that they had been paid. If they had not,
Serena did not know how she would be able to look the
said tradesmen in the face.

"Perhaps the need to be practical will give your mother's
thoughts a new direction," Miss Abbott said, though without conviction.

When Thursday came, her mother did indeed make the
supreme effort.

"My dear, I must. It is what your poor father would have
wished," she said resolutely as she sat draped in a great
many shawls beside the fire in the morning room, her vinaigrette within reach on the small side table.

The firm of Price, Witherspoon, and Price, in Wilton,
had always dealt with Papa's affairs, but the older Price had
now retired, leaving his son to take over the business. He
arrived promptly, and Serena's fears were immediately set
at rest, for he was very much a younger version of his father, with the same beaky nose and bushy eyebrows, and
quiet reassuring demeanor. And, having been plied with a
glass of Madeira, he was embarrassed rather than pompous
as he patiently answered all her mother's kindly inquiries
concerning his father, before endeavoring to explain to her
that the monies paid regularly into her household account
during her husband's lifetime would not in future be forth-
coming.

"Well, naturally, one would not expect the army . . ." her voice faltered. "But Elliott will have made provision . . ."

Mr. Price paused to direct an almost pleading glance at Serena before adding that when her mother's late husband's outstanding debts had been settled, the only regular source of income would derive from a modest jointure, which had been securely tied up by Mr. Price, senior, some years previously.

"A jointure!" Mrs. Fairburn seized on the word with relief as she reached for her smelling bottle. "There, Serena, did I not tell you that your father would do everything that was proper?"

Serena noticed in an almost detached way that little beads of perspiration were forming along Mr. Price's upper lip, and that the pleading look had become more urgent.

"Quite so, Mama. But you are looking tired. Perhaps now that your mind is at rest, you would like me to ring the bell, and Parkin shall take you back to your room. You may safely leave me to settle all the tiresome details. I'm sure Mr. Price will understand . . ."

"Yes, indeed," he said hastily, relief mingling with embarrassment.

"So good, dear child . . . so kind . . ." Parkin came in at this point and gathered up her charge. "Thank you so much for coming, Mr. Price," Mrs. Fairburn said graciously. "As you can see"—she patted Serena's hand—"I am blessed with a wonderful daughter."

There was an awkward silence in the room when the door closed behind her. But Serena did not allow it to stretch, lest her courage should desert her.

"I see you understand my problem, Mr. Price," she said in her forthright way. "However, I am not a fool or missish, so be plain with me, if you please. How badly are we placed?"

He moved uncomfortably. "Is there no one—a male relation of some kind who might . . . ?"

"Only my brother, Connaught. I have written to him, of course, but he is somewhere in France with the Army of Occupation —which is perhaps as well, since his understanding of money matters is little better than Mama's."

Mr. Price looked shocked at such plain speaking, but in the end he reluctantly gave her chapter and verse. Serena did not immediately grasp the finer points, but the gist of the matter seemed to be that for the moment there was no fear of them being turned out into the street, though he could not guarantee that there would be any appreciable funds in the bank when all had been accounted for. Also— he coughed nervously—a loan taken out by the colonel some years ago presented an added complication.

"I daresay he had meant to settle it long since, but the thing is, under the terms agreed at the time, that will now be called in. I am not as yet sure how best to deal with it. Aside from the jointure, I'm afraid your father resisted all advice to tie up sufficient extra monies to cover such eventualities"—he cleared his throat again "—or indeed to provide more adequately for his family in the event of his . . ."

As Serena listened, she found herself in the grip of a quite un-Christian anger as she began to realize Papa's shocking want of thought.

"His dealings at that time, of course, were with my own father, who tells me that the colonel's optimism was such that he refused to regard the possibility that a time might come when he would not return, as always, richer in prize monies than when he left."

How like Papa! Serena was on the point of wondering how she was to explain to her mother that Harry's fees for Eton would be forfeit, and likewise Edward's chances of exchanging the tender administrations of their dear Miss

Abbott to follow in his steps, when Mr. Price began to speak again.

"It is, I believe, sometimes the case with military men. They lose touch with the realities of everyday life. However, in his last communication to my father, just before he left for Brussels, the colonel did intimate that he had, he hoped, arranged matters advantageously for your future, Miss Serena"—he looked for confirmation, but saw only blank mystification, and so concluded lamely—"he seemed to feel that your imminent betrothal would inevitably overcome any future pecuniary embarrassment."

"My what?" For a moment the room spun. Then common sense reasserted itself. She said with a humor born of desperation, "I'm sorry, Mr. Price. You must have misunderstood—would that you had not. There is, to my knowledge, no such betrothal, not even a mildly interested suitor."

He frowned. "How very odd. I don't have the letter with me, but I will look it up when I return to Wilton. As I recall, he touched upon the matter but lightly. I wonder . . ." he suggested diffidently. "Would the colonel have communicated his intentions more fully to Mrs. Fairburn?"

"Oh, no, he cannot have done; Mama would have been sure to mention any such possibility to me." Thoroughly confused by now, Serena could hardly wait for Mr. Price to take his leave so that she might rush upstairs to see what she could discover if indeed there was anything to be discovered, which she doubted.

But go he did, at last, carrying a box full of documents. "Let us not despair so soon, Miss Fairburn," he said with forced cheerfulness, promising to be in touch with the utmost speed.

Serena found her mother amazingly buoyed up by Mr. Price's visit, convinced that all would now be well, and she decided that no purpose would be served by pricking the bubble of her complacency until it became absolutely necessary.

"Do you recall, Mama," she began as casually as she could manage, "whether Papa ever mentioned, however slightly, any plans he might have envisioned for my future?"

"Plans? What kind of plans, dearest? I know he always wanted the very best for you, for you all . . ." Suddenly, she seemed to hold her breath, a frown creased her brow, and she sat up with a start, her smelling bottle cast aside, her pretty black lace cap knocked askew on her soft gray curls. "Oh, my dear child, I had quite forgotten!"

"Forgotten what, Mama?"

"It was . . . oh, quickly, do pray fetch me the box in which I keep your father's letters. It was the very last one I received from Brussels, some time before . . ." Here her feelings threatened to overcome her. But curiosity proved to be a more powerful incentive as Serena put the pretty ormulu box into her hands. The search should not take long, for there were few enough letters for all the years of absence.

"Your father stayed a night at Masham Court with the Duchess of Cornwell when he left that last time as I recall," her mama continued tearfully, her trembling fingers scrabbling among the pages, "though why he should have wished to do so when he could have remained longer with us . . . except that Masham is near enough to Portsmouth for him to stay a night there . . . and he is . . . was distantly related to the duchess, who is, of course, a Fairburn. . . ."

Serena was on the point of screaming by the time Mama found the letter and tearfully perused it.

"Oh, will you read it aloud, my dear, for I cannot

bear . . ." She pointed a shaky finger. "Somewhere about here, I believe."

Serena read slowly and clearly.

I found Her Grace very troubled. Cedric being her only child, and sickly to boot, she has always kept him secure at home. But the young duke has already had one brush with death this last winter, and she is now haunted by the knowledge that if he should die without issue, the estate will be broken up and divided amongst the remainder of the family. Such a course would be a severe blow to her pride, so she now looks for a suitable bride. Naturally I seized the opportunity to suggest a possible match with our dear Serena—you must remember Her Grace's extraordinary pride in the Fairburn name—and she seemed more than a little interested. So who knows, my love, but that something may come of it and your daughter may yet be a duchess! You would like that, I believe. And now . . .

Here the letter became personal, and Serena hurriedly put it back in her mother's hand.

Serena's first reaction was one of revulsion that any woman should put love of power beyond any risk to her son's health. But this was quickly followed by a quite unreasoning rage that her father had acted with a similar want of consideration.

"How could he? Without so much as a word to me!" she cried as indignation overcame prudence. "As if I were a commodity to be bartered!"

"Dear child, don't." Mrs. Fairburn dabbed her eyes, much overcome by hearing her husband's last words read aloud to her. "Papa will have had your best interests at heart. One cannot blame him for thinking it an excellent match, which it undoubtedly is. I met Her Grace but once and confess that I found her more than a trifle . . ." She paused, bit her lip, and continued resolutely, "However, that is not to say that her son would not be quite charming. Oh dearest, only think—our problems would be solved at a stroke. I am not quite a fool, and I know things are not quite as they should be. But of course I would not try to force you . . . If only we may not be cast out into the street!" At this last Mrs. Fairburn's voice broke on a sob.

"Mama, don't!" Serena swallowed her anger, ashamed that she had so far forgotten her mother's delicate condition. "I'm sure Mr. Price would not let it come to that. As for Papa's talk of betrothals—it is all very vague. I think we must just wait and see."

As the weeks passed without word from the duchess, Serena hardly knew whether to be glad or sorry—especially when Mr. Price finally confirmed to her the serious nature of their finances. It seemed that these would just about cover the minimum required to meet all outstanding debts, including the repayment of the loan, thus leaving Mama's jointure as the family's sole source of income.

She wished with all her heart that it was a bad dream from which she would presently awaken while knowing full well that it was not, and wondering however she was to break the news to Mama. If only Connaught would come. At least then the burden would be shared.

"Does this mean that we shall have to sell the Grange?" Serena asked Mr. Price.

"That would certainly be the most straightforward way of settling the matter. For one thing, a smaller establishment would be less costly to maintain." He pulled out a neatly folded handkerchief and mopped his brow. "Oh, dear, this is really very difficult. I suppose you have learned nothing further concerning that other matter we spoke of— the possibility of a betrothal?"

He was clearly embarrassed, but she felt quite unable to explain it in any detail, saying merely that the idea was so vague that it was unlikely to amount to anything.

"A pity. However, let us not despair. We will leave any decision concerning the house aside for the moment," he continued, "and look for economies in the short term. How many servants do you have at present?"

Serena's heart plummeted still further. "There is Cook and Ruby and a general maid. And Parkin, of course— Mama could not manage without Parkin. And there is George, who looks after the gardens and the stable. Oh, but we can't turn any of them off! They have been with us forever and are like family . . ."

His expression silenced her.

"And the governess?"

"Oh, surely not Miss Abbott?" she pleaded.

"I am sorry, Miss Fairburn. But we must consider all possibilities. Even if their wages are cut to the bone, these people will still have to be fed and housed. Which means that painful decisions must be taken as to who goes and who stays. And then there is the matter of your brother's schooling."

Ah, poor Harry! "Yes, I do accept that we cannot hope to keep Harry at Eton." Serena suddenly felt very tired. "Will you give me a little time to . . . to think, and to break the news to Mama and the family?"

"Yes, of course." He hesitated, then said earnestly, "This is not easy for me, either, Miss Fairburn. But the sooner the thing is done, the sooner you may begin to take stock."

She had already spent precious hours doing so, and there was one way in which she might be able to stave off the inevitable for a while longer.

"Mr. Price, how much would it take to pay off the loan?"

He seemed taken aback by the question and was obliged

to consult his papers. "Something in the region of one hundred and fifty pounds."

Serena let out the breath she had been holding. "Well then." She reached into her pocket and drew out a long, slim box and pressed the catch. "This rope of pearls was given to me by my maternal grandmother. They are quite good ones, I believe."

Dear Grandmother Bradstock, whom she had loved so much, and who had shocked everyone in her latter years by entering into a second and very happy marriage with a bluff self-made man, a rich cotton merchant. When she had visited Mountford shortly before her death, she had given Serena the pearls, confiding to her alone that should a time ever come when she had need of money, they would provide excellent collateral.

Serena would be sad to part with the pearls, for they had been given with love. Mama had thought them quite pretty, very suitable for a young girl, though she had no idea of their worth.

Mr. Price stared down at their milky translucence, each one perfectly matched. He was no expert, of course, but . . . "Miss Fairburn, I do not know quite what you intend, but I really do not think you should . . ."

"They are mine to do with as I will," she assured him, adding resolutely, "and I have every reason to believe that if they were sold, the amount raised would more than cover Papa's debts and leave us something to spare. I could perhaps buy a much cheaper rope, and that way Mama need never know. The only problem is, I haven't the slightest idea how to go about it."

"No more have I," he admitted with refreshing frankness. "I suppose I could make inquiries—if you are quite sure? They are very beautiful, and I would hazard, quite irreplaceable."

"I am quite sure."

He placed the pearls almost reverently in their box and put them in his case. "You realize that this will solve nothing in the long term?"

"No, but it will buy us time." Her smile had a hint of bravura. "And miracles do occasionally happen. Connaught might yet arrive home with the news that he has married an heiress."

Mr. Price picked up his hat, opened his mouth, shut it again, and then, rather red in the face, said in a rush, "May I tell you, Miss Fairburn, how very much I admire your strength and courage—to say nothing of your devotion to your family."

She hardly knew how to answer. But in the event, he seemed suddenly anxious to leave, and she was spared the necessity.

Some days later, when she was on her way to sort the linen, Edward came charging up the stairs and ran full into her.

"There's a gentleman called to see Mama!" he panted. "A real lord, as fine as fivepence! You should see his curricle—all black and shiny with huge yellow wheels and two splendid horses! And a boy no bigger than me standing up behind in gold livery—"

Serena's heart began to thud. "Teddy! Stop at once and begin again."

Emily, who had heard most of her brother's garbled message, seized hold of him, her cerulean eyes huge. "Did you say a lord?"

"That's what he told Ruby. She's shown him into the parlor," he said, drawing breath.

By this time Ruby had labored up the stairs to give her own version of events in a dramatic whisper, her eyes very round. "Ever so grand he is, Miss Serena. Come with a message, he said, from 'is aunt, who's a duchess! 'Give me 'is card, 'e did."

Serena felt her heart turn over in her breast as she glanced at the card that proclaimed their visitor to be the Earl of Lynton.

No one would have guessed that Serena's mind was in turmoil as she said calmly, "Thank you, Ruby. I will come down at once. Teddy, run along to the nursery and stay there." She turned to Emily. "Will you be so kind as to go and tell Mama that she has a visitor, and without your partiality for high drama, if you please. I will entertain him until Parkin brings her down."

Emily's mouth took a stubborn line. It wasn't fair that she should be deprived of meeting Mama's prestigious guest. "Why can't Ruby tell her, then I could come with you?"

"Because Ruby would fluster Mama."

"So would I, you know I would!" Emily fell to wheedling. "It would really be best if you told her. I could go down and entertain—"

"Certainly not." Serena's voice was sharper than she had intended. "Oh, Emily, don't make difficulties, please! And try not to rush Mama or agitate her in any way."

With relief, she saw Abby come from the nursery and swiftly explained. The governess subdued her own curiosity and took charge.

"Come along, now, Emily, I'll accompany you. Two heads are better than one."

Rebellion flared momentarily, then Emily flounced away, followed by the neat unruffled figure of Miss Abbott, and Serena made her way slowly down the stairs.

On the hall stand near the door a high-crowned beaver hat held pride of place, as if to mock her.

" 'E wouldn't give me 'is coat," Ruby whispered loud enough for the whole house to hear. "If you could call what 'e's wearin' a coat!"

"Hush, Ruby!"

Outside the drawing room Serena paused to smooth down her black crepe gown, wishing it could have been something less stark—more becoming. To know that one looked one's best might at least give her confidence. She drew a deep breath, straightened her back, and opened the door.

A figure in a long drab coat of many capes seemed to fill the window embrasure. As the door clicked, he turned, and she was at once aware of hard, dark eyes beneath black brows, of swirling black hair, a face sculpted by planes and angles, and a mouth that was at once sensuous and unyielding. His coat fell back to reveal polished top boots coated with a fine layer of dust, and above them, close-fitting buff breeches that betrayed the strength of muscle in his long legs.

Not to be outdone, he lifted an eyeglass on a plain black riband, and she found herself being subject to an unhurried and equally detailed appraisal.

Chapter Two

Darcy, sixth Earl of Lynton, had not relished the task laid upon him by his aunt. But one did not, without pause, attempt to thwart Her Grace. Also, if he was honest, he was curious to see what kind of creature was like to be foisted upon Cousin Cedric as his loving bride.

His immediate thought was that the tall, slim young woman standing now with her back to the door as if protecting her line of retreat, and watching him with a mixture of pride and trepidation, had little by way of looks to recommend her. Which was, of itself, surprising, for the late lamented Colonel Fairburn had been flamboyantly handsome.

"Miss Fairburn?" he inquired with exquisite irony when she did not speak, and made her a bow. "I am Lynton."

Serena had been guilty of staring and came to with a start, a faint blush staining her cheeks as she realized how gauche, how lacking in manners she must appear. Nevertheless, she made herself meet his slate gray eyes with composure.

"Yes, of course. My lord, forgive me, I had not expected . . ."

She walked forward with a polite smile, conscious as never before, of the shabbiness of the furnishings. He made no attempt to offer his hand, and she was unsure whether etiquette demanded that she should make the first move. In the end she decided against it, saying merely, "Do, pray be seated. I believe you will find that chair comfortable. It was the one my father was used to favor. May I offer you some refreshment—a glass of Madeira, perhaps?"

He declined, a glint of something that was not quite humor in his cool inquisitorial gaze, and with punctilious politeness remained standing until she herself was seated.

"Mama will be down directly," she said, making a determined effort to converse. "She has taken my father's death badly, so I would ask you to"—she paused, aware that what she had been about to say might be construed as less than tactful—"to bear that in mind," she concluded lamely.

The earl inclined his head, and she knew he had divined her thoughts. When he spoke, however, it was merely to say with deceptive blandness, "And is Miss Fairburn equally grief-stricken?"

Serena could feel the color creep into her cheeks again. But her chin came up and her eyes met his squarely. "If I said yes, you would not believe me, I think. I am very sad, of course. But we saw Papa so seldom—it is different for Mama."

"An honest answer." His mouth quirked sardonically. "Interesting." His voice grew silky. "I wonder would you be as honest if I asked you how you felt about becoming a duchess?"

Confusion turned to indignation, but before she could reply, the door opened to admit Mama, who was accompanied by Emily instead of Parkin, which did not surprise her, but proved to be an added irritant. She performed the introductions, and Emily shot her a triumphant look before dipping a formal little curtsy that Serena recognized as being taken straight from the pages of the *Lady's Monthly Mu-*

seum, and turning the full force of her charm on his lordship. He was politeness itself, but Serena was further mortified to see how the curl of his lip mirrored his thoughts.

However, his behavior toward Mama could not be
faulted as he rose to express his sympathy with a simple
sincerity that almost convinced Serena he meant every
word—not least his assertion that he had had the honor of
knowing and liking Colonel Fairburn. He could not have
said anything more guaranteed to please Mama, though the
tears, never far away, trembled on her lashes. And for that
at least, Serena must be grateful.

While Mama dabbed at her eyes with an inadequate
square of embroidered cambric, he explained that as his
own country retreat lay within a mile or two of Mountford,
he had offered to be the duchess's messenger.

"Pray do not attempt to read this now," he said, putting
into her hands the letter bearing a crest and an impressive
seal. There was a curious lack of expression in his voice as
he added, "Her Grace has charged me to say that, anxious
as she is to learn of your reaction to her proposition, you
must take such time as you need for consideration."

So the contents were known to him. Serena's cheeks
burned.

The earl bowed. "And now, I must bid you good day."

"Oh, but you must let us offer you some refreshment, my
lord!" Mrs. Fairburn cried, not wishing to see so elegant a
creature depart her home with such speed. "Serena, what
can you be thinking of . . . ?"

"Miss Fairburn has said and done everything that is
proper, ma'am," he said smoothly. "But, sadly, I must de-
cline. My horses are high-couraged cattle, and they grow
restive if they are obliged to stand for any length of time."
He bowed. "Your servant, ma'am, Miss Fairburn, Miss
Emily."

"I'll bring your hat, my lord," Emily said demurely, rising with grace and gliding to the door, ignoring Serena's quick frown. She returned, hat reverently in hand, subjecting him to yet another curtsy and peeping up at him through her long lashes as she offered it to him.

"You are too kind, Miss Emily."

Serena could have told him that the irony in his voice would be quite lost on her sister. Yet, as she accompanied him into the hall, she was meticulous in thanking him for taking the trouble to call on her mother personally with the letter.

"It was no trouble, Miss Fairburn," he assured her, "No doubt we shall meet again in the not too distant future."

"Do you think so?" Serena refused to be drawn into any kind of commitment. "You posed a question to me earlier, my lord," she said, opening the door. "The answer is quite simple. As I presently entertain no expectation of becoming a duchess, any feelings I might have would seem to be irrelevant."

A hardness crept into his eyes. "So that is to be the way of it? Well, we shall see, Miss Fairburn." He paused on the step to accord her the briefest of bows before setting his beaver hat firmly on his head. "Your servant, ma'am."

His cutting formality was somewhat ruined by a skirmish on the front drive, and the sound of the young tiger's raised voice, shrill with outrage.

"These is prime tits—not ter be trifled wiv by some bleedin' little tike who ain't got the first idea how ter treat 'em!"

Edward had managed to evade Abby's eagle eye and creep down the back stairs. Thence, he had made his way by stealth to the front of the house where he was presently subjecting Lord Lynton's curricle and pair to an overenthusiastic examination, which was causing his lordship's horses to back restively and show the whites of their eyes, so that the young tiger had his work cut out to hold them.

"I do, too, know how!" Edward shouted back with a fine disregard for the truth. "My brother Connaught once had a rig every bit as fine."

"Edward, come here at once."

"But . . ."

"At once, Edward."

When Serena used that tone, you didn't argue. Females never understood. He turned with dragging step, aggrieved that he was to be blamed for something that wasn't his fault. "I didn't *mean* to excite the horses . . ."

"I've told you, them's not just 'orses, bone-head . . ."

"Jack." The earl did not raise his voice, but the young tiger immediately closed his mouth on the crushing retort he had been about to deliver. "Pray do not make bad worse by indulging in vulgar abuse."

"That's all very well, Guv," he muttered, his small frame straining to hang on to his charges. "But there's some as need tellin' what's what."

"Not by you, I think," came the cold reply. "You will oblige me by doing what I pay you to do, and no more."

"If you say so, Guv. In which case, it's time we was orf, fer I can't hold 'em much longer."

Serena was so astonished by the amount of license granted by the earl to this strange little monkey of a creature, that for once she chose not to exact an apology from Edward. It seemed however that none was expected, for with a curt nod of the head, his lordship strode toward his curricle, leaped up lightly, and took up his reins and his whip.

"Right, Jack, let them go," he commanded.

As the horses plunged forward, the tiger leaped nimbly out of their path to run and swing himself up behind. A swift blast on the horn and the equipage departed in a cloud of dust, his lordship judging the width of the gateposts to a nicety.

"I say!" breathed Edward.

Serena would like to have said something scathing about such people being a menace on the roads, but in truth she could not but admire the skill with which Lord Lynton had executed the turn into the roadway.

In the parlor she found Emily urging her mother to open the letter.

"Just wait until I tell Jane Summerton. I vow, she will be green with envy, for I cannot imagine her mama ever had a letter from anyone half so important as a duchess!"

"Emily, don't tease Mama," Serena said quietly. "You will likely bring on one of her migraines. Go and ask Ruby to prepare one of her special tisanes."

"But . . ."

"No 'buts,' I beg of you. You shall know all in good time."

For a moment it seemed that her sister would refuse, but in the end she left, muttering about sisters who spoiled sport.

"You do not have to open the letter immediately, Mama. Lord Lynton said you were to take your time."

"Yes, dear, but I shall not rest until I *know*." She lifted the letter with trembling fingers and broke the seal, and feverishly scanned the page. "Her Grace offers her commiserations . . . and, yes . . . your father's suggestion must have found favor . . . at least, she wishes us to visit Masham Court. She even condescends to send her carriage for us. Oh, Serena, only think what this must mean!"

Serena *was* thinking. It meant the possibility of her marrying—at best, an invalid—at worst . . . her mind refused to contemplate the alternative. Her faith in the power of prayer severely tested, she was slow to answer. The clock on the mantelshelf ticked relentlessly as her mother awaited her answer.

"Of course, if it is truly not what you would like . . ."

Mama's voice held no note of criticism, yet Serena knew as Mrs. Fairburn did not, just how much depended on her answer. What she would *like*—what every young woman would surely like—was to be courted by a dashing and highly eligible young man who would fall madly in love with her and sweep her off her feet.

But where was she to find such a young man in Mountford Tracy? Or anywhere else, for that matter?

"I suppose we could at least go to Masham," she conceded with as good a grace as she could muster. "But I think we will say nothing to the others concerning the true purpose of the visit. It would be so embarrassing for me if all came to nought."

In the days that followed, the house was in turmoil as preparations for the visit were made. Mama had two black crepe day gowns, and various shawls, but ordered a new bombazine gown for evenings from Miss Hoare, the village dressmaker, who was only too happy to oblige, the outstanding account having been recently settled.

Serena had already dyed several of her muslin day gowns, and had trimmed her lilac sarcenet with black ribbon.

"I really think that should suffice," she told Abby, who had come looking for her, and had found her sitting on her bed, morosely surveying her limited wardrobe. The governess had suggested in her quiet practical way that a new evening gown might not be considered an extravagance for such an important visit.

"My dear, if you wish to create a good impression, I do think a little expenditure would pay dividends."

"I'm not entirely sure that I do wish to create a good impression," she retorted in an unguarded moment. Then she added: "I'm sorry, Abby. You mustn't mind my stupid megrims."

Miss Abbott watched the color come and go in her face. She had not been blind to all the comings and goings, and the drawn look on the countenance of this, her favorite of all the Fairburn offspring.

A certain urgency led her to venture further. "My dear, I would have to be blind to have remained unaware of the stress under which you have been laboring these weeks past. If it would help to talk?"

"Oh, Abby, there is little point to talking, but I own it would ease my mind to unburden myself . . . are the children . . . ?"

"All safely occupied. Mary is painting a picture, Edward has gone across to the rectory for his Latin lesson with Mr. Gray, and Emily is out walking with Jane Summerton."

So Serena confided the whole of her problem to Miss Abbott, who listened with quiet composure, not by so much as a flicker betraying her anger that Serena should be subjected to so much responsibility.

"And is there really no other way?" was all she said.

Serena shook her head.

"Even if the outstanding debt can be cleared, it will not alter the fact that our long-term position is, to say the least, gloomy. Naturally, I have said nothing to Mama, although I believe she has guessed that all is not quite as it should be."

An understatement, by any reckoning, thought the governess with sudden anger. A girl of eighteen should not be expected to bear so much alone. To her way of thinking, it was high time Mrs. Fairburn pulled herself together. And as for Connaught, who was now the man of the family . . . the least he could do would be to sell out and come home to take charge. But then young men were ever thoughtless, and he was very like his father.

She said, almost casually, "As you must be aware, my dear, I have been here for so long that I am sometimes tempted to consider myself as a member of the family . . ."

"Oh, but you are! The dearest and best of members. Why, I cannot remember a time when you were not here!"

"You are a good, kind girl," said Miss Abbott, much moved. "And your opinion encourages me to make a suggestion. When I was young, I had a dream—that in my old age I would retire and either travel the Continent, seeing all the places I have always longed to see, or buy myself a little cottage somewhere in the country where I could sit in the sun and grow roses."

Serena was momentarily taken out of her misery by this entrancingly new and unexpected image of the rather prosaic woman who had for so long been their guide and mentor.

"To which end I put aside a certain amount of money each year. I have long since realized of course that my funds would be quite inadequate for the former, and the latter would fill me with ennui in no time at all." She smiled self-depreciatingly. "In short, what I am saying is that I have some five hundred pounds saved, and if it would be of any use in helping you out of this wretched situation, then I would consider it a privilege to make it available to you on whatever terms your solicitor thinks appropriate."

There was a momentary silence, and then Serena burst into tears.

"My dear! Pray forgive me! The last thing I would wish is to upset you in any way."

"You haven't . . . it isn't . . ." She flung her arms around the older woman, her head against the firm unyielding bosom. "Oh, Abby, you are such a dear!"

"There, now, child." Abby patted her awkwardly. "Don't take on so. It's only money."

"I can't accept, of course." Serena sat back at last, dabbing at her eyes with a handkerchief. "But your offer has quite restored my spirits."

"Then I see no reason why you should refuse my offer," the governess said mildly. "As long as I am guaranteed a roof over my head for such time as you need the money, I shall be well content."

Serena drew a deep breath. "But, you see, it wouldn't answer, not in the long term, and that, I fear, is what is needed. So, for now, it seems, the duchess is our best hope."

Chapter Three

S tand up straight, gel," commanded the Dowager
Duchess of Cornwell, her pince-nez hovering above a
bony nose. "And closer to the window, if you please, where
I may better see you."

For all the world, Serena thought indignantly, as if I were
a prize mare. In a moment she will be wishing to feel my
hocks and examine my teeth, and that will be too much!

She intercepted a despairing glance from her mama and
swallowed her wrath, for indeed the statuesque duchess in
her deep purple bombazine gown and feathered toque,
which made no concessions to the current fashion for high
waists and narrow skirts, was imposing enough to induce
palpitations in persons blessed with far stouter constitutions
than Mama.

Poor Mama. She looked nervous and desperately frail in
her blacks. This was as much an indignity for her—more
so, perhaps—for it must always be a painful and demeaning
experience to be obliged to sacrifice one's offspring upon
the altar of Mammon.

It had been a long and tiring journey, even allowing for
an overnight stop and all the comforts provided by the
Cornwell traveling coach, with its outriders and postillions,
sent to carry them from Wiltshire to the duke's country seat
near Winchester. Parkin did not travel well, and only an

overriding concern for her mistress enabled her to bear up. Their first sight of Masham Court had done little to cheer any of them, for even at a distance, its proportions were not elegant.

She had felt her mama's resolve begin to crumble as the butler, Westerby, receiving them austerely, announced that Her Grace would receive them in the Crimson Salon, and dispatched Parkin to accompany the baggage, before ushering them through the echoing hall toward the great carved staircase, which divided on a half landing dominated by a huge stained glass window. The second flight led to a wide gallery, paneled in dark oak, that appeared to stretch into infinity on either side. Westerby unerringly turned left, his measured tread adjusting to their own smaller steps.

In an attempt to make light of their inhospitable surroundings, Serena had murmured irrepressibly that it was exactly the sort of house that must have inspired Mrs. Radclyffe to put pen to paper, for she would own herself very much astonished if there were not at least one ghostly apparition doomed to walk the passages.

Mama's smile had been so bravely attempted that Serena could have wept with anger and frustration. She had hoped against hope that a warm welcome might cancel out these first impressions, but any hope of improvement was dashed the moment they entered the vast gloomy salon with its heavy Jacobean furniture, its thick velvet curtains, and walls covered in wine-colored brocade, to be confronted by the overpowering presence of the duchess, who greeted them, sitting bolt upright in a chair more reminiscent of a throne, set to one side of a cavernous fireplace.

"You are a trifle on the tall side, are you not, Miss Fairburn?" The reedy voice commanded her attention once more. "A pity, but it cannot be helped," she added ambiguously. "Your bonnet, child. Remove your bonnet, if you please. Black is not a young gel's color, and plain as it is, does little to improve your looks."

As if I were in mourning from choice. Serena's fingers shook uncontrollably as they tugged at the hateful black ribbons.

"To be sure, Mrs. Fairburn, eighteen is rather younger than I had hoped for . . ."

"I shall be nineteen at Christmas," Serena said quickly, earning herself a frown.

The voice ran on as though there had been no interruption. "Though, on reflection, it might be for the best. The character is still amenable to correction—and the vital question, that of breeding, cannot be faulted." The duchess's chin lifted with regal pride. "The Fairburns, as you must be aware, are among the earlier and most prestigious families in England—in which respect they far outstrip my late husband's family, the Ruffords, who only came to prominence during the Reformation, when the dukedom was created. The colonel, of course, whilst having inherited all the Fairburn family's most agreeable traits, belonged to a lesser branch. Though, had he lived, he would have been third in line to succeed the earl, my father. However, that it is of little consequence now."

Mrs. Fairburn uttered a muffled sound and pressed a handkerchief to her mouth, her voice but a thread. "My poor Elliott! Torn from me . . . and just when we all thought that monster, Napoleon, vanquished!"

"Quite so. But we must not . . ."

"The Duke of Wellington wrote personally to tell me of my husband's great bravery at Quatre Bras . . ." Mrs. Fairburn's voice failed at last and trailed away.

"Yes, yes, the colonel was indeed brave. A charming man—everything one would expect in a soldier, and I'm sure he behaved exactly as he should. Still, it don't do to dwell on what is past and gone."

A choked sound was the only reply. The duchess, Serena thought savagely, is an unfeeling monster. Once more, the need to protect her mother threatened to overcome all her resolve. In an attempt to draw the duchess's fire, she said stiffly, "Mama was particularly devoted to my father."

"So it would appear." The awesome gaze became focused upon her once more. "You have dark hair, I see." A note of disapproval entered the bombastic voice. "I trust I do not detect not a trace of red in it? There is something distinctly unsettling about red hair. Your father was fair, of course. The Fairburn men have always been flaxen-haired. Your brothers will have maintained the tradition, I daresay?"

Serena could not bring herself to answer, though no reply seemed to be expected of her, since the duchess had the curious habit of posing questions without ever expecting or indeed inviting an answer.

"I am pleased to say that my poor Cedric follows my side of the family in looks," she swept on. "He was a late child and has been delicate from birth, as the colonel no doubt explained to you. Also, a continuing weakness of the heart gives cause for concern. That is why the choice of a wife is of paramount importance. She must possess a steady and caring nature. Some flighty young miss, forever kicking up starts, and wishing to attend balls and the like, would never do."

"Had I been blessed with other sons," Her Grace continued with hardly a pause for breath, "I would on no account have countenanced his entering into the married state. But if the line is to be preserved, it must be attempted. The Fairburns have never shirked a challenge, and in this instance affection for my only child must be sacrificed to the greater good. I have told Cedric that it is his duty, insofar as circumstances allow, to father an heir. Our doctor assures me that, with care, it can be managed."

An outrageous prospect! Serena almost rebelled there and then, but the voice was already sweeping on.

"It was providential that my cousin, Major Newsham, should have brought your husband to Masham for the weekend just before they left for Brussels. Colonel Fairburn suggested to me that his eldest daughter might be the ideal wife for Cedric, making much of her steadfast nature"—here a frowning glance was directed at Serena. "Unfortunately there was no time for formal arrangements to be completed, but as he will no doubt have communicated to you, he was very much in favor of the match."

Oh, he was! Serena felt again that sense of having been betrayed. Had she been consulted, she would not willingly have contemplated taking to husband any man so sickly and poor spirited as to allow himself to be bullied into marriage by his mother, merely for the sake of perpetuating the family name.

But this, she swiftly recollected, was not for herself. It was for Emily, and Harry, and Edward, and little Mary. And for her mother, who would be financially secure for the remainder of her life.

"Serena is a most generous-natured girl," ventured Mrs. Fairburn, her gentle despairing voice breaking slightly as she added, "I do not know how I should have gone on without her these past weeks. She has been a tower of strength since . . . I fear Elliott left his affairs in something of a tangle . . ." her voice sank and rose again. "Our lawyer, Mr. Price, has been most helpful, but business matter are so confusing . . . and with dear Connaught, my eldest son, somewhere in France . . . I know not where, Serena has dealt with it all . . ."

Here the words finally became choked and incoherent, and she groped for her reticule.

Serena ignored the duchess's impatient "tch" as she moved swiftly to her mother's side, and in a calm practical way extracted the vinaigrette from her mother's reticule and pressed it into her hand.

"So good, dear child . . . so kind . . ."

For a woman impatient of any tendency in her own sex to succumb to the vapors, the duchess watched the scene with remarkable complacence. Miss Fairburn showed a cool head in the face of illness, which was much in her favor. There was a shade too much spirit there, but that could be corrected. Her bombazine skirts rustled.

"Very commendable, ma'am. It will no doubt be a consolation to you to know that, should your daughter, on further acquaintance, prove to possess those qualities essential to any future Duchess of Cornwell, your problems will be at an end. And Miss Fairburn will be making an infinitely better match than she could possibly have looked for in the ordinary way. For, although not entirely ill-favored, her circumstances must surely have precluded her from achieving any appreciable success on the marriage mart."

Serena knew she must escape soon, or say something extremely unwise. Deliverance came unexpectedly from the duchess herself who announced almost graciously that Pennyweather would presently take them to their rooms to refresh themselves and rest until it was time for tea to be served.

"However, perhaps you would first care to take your mother for a brief stroll in the garden, Miss Fairburn, so that she may recover herself a little? Tea is taken at four o'clock, when I trust my son may be present to make your acquaintance. Cedric occupies a suite of rooms on the ground floor facing the south terrace, so that he is not forever climbing the stairs."

Mrs. Fairburn's eyes kindled at the thought of tea.

"Pennyweather!" the peremptory voice commanded, and a wraithlike figure wrapped in shawls, who had been completely unnoticed until that moment, and was introduced briefly as a distant relation, scuttled from a corner furthest from the fire. "Pennyweather, pray open the doors leading out to the garden."

The little dab of a woman smiled nervously, murmured, "Yes, indeed, Elvira, at once," and, clutching at her shawls, hurried to do the duchess's bidding. Serena took her mother's arm gently, and they followed her to the huge expanse of window, where their progress faltered as the central doors were thrown open.

"I'm not sure, dear, if I . . ." Mrs. Fairburn was clearly torn between making an effort that was almost beyond her, or remaining a moment longer in the company of her overpowering cousin by marriage. However, the sight of the long iron-balustraded flight of steps leading down to the gardens proved too much for her resolve.

"Oh, no. I really could not attempt . . ." Serena's heart plummeted. "But you go along, dear. I shall do much better to go to my room at once. Parkin will have made everything ready for me, I'm sure, and I can rest quietly until teatime."

Rebellion, an unfamiliar emotion, was uppermost in Serena's breast as she hurried down the steps to the paved courtyard below and from there took a pathway leading away from the house toward a terraced garden beyond. Halfway, she turned and looked back.

If that first glimpse of Masham Court from the carriage had oppressed Serena with its sheer size and ugliness, at close quarters it proved every bit as ugly. She stared up at the massive west front with its rows of windows like hostile eyes winking back at her, and found herself longing for the use of Edward's catapult. The idea caused her mouth to curve in amusement. But within moments the exigencies of her present situation returned to frustrate her.

The more she heard about Cedric, the more apprehensive she became.

Suppose, only suppose, she had ventured to Abby the night before leaving home, that he were some kind of backward creature?

Abby, reassuring her, had thought it most unlikely, and at any other time Serena would have dismissed her fears. But, with the demons of the night closing in, reason had for once deserted her.

"I couldn't do it, Abby—not even for Mama's sake! Not if he were as rich as Croesus," she had cried in despair, "could I engage to marry an idiot!"

But as Abby had reasonably pointed out, her father was acquainted with the young man and would not have countenanced any such match.

She was right, of course, Serena thought. And now, in the clear light of day, any such assumption seemed absurd. The duchess had spoken of a delicate constitution caused by a weak heart, nothing more. At worst, Cedric, Fourth Duke of Cornwell, would likely prove to be no more than an ineffectual young man, very much under his mother's thumb. And, viewed logically, there must be worse fates than marrying a moral weakling.

She had been walking aimlessly, without regard for her surroundings. Now she saw that her steps had led her round on to a different terrace that looked out over beds of sweet-smelling herbs of all kinds, with rose gardens beyond and lawns of lush green velvet spreading away to meet the encompassing woodland in the distance.

She drew a deep breath in which was all the fragrance of a summer's day, not looking where she was going until, looking down, she stood still with a muttered exclamation.

In another moment she would have tripped over a slim young man lying prone upon the path. Was he ill—injured? Perhaps dead? None of these things, apparently, for he said, "Hush," very softly and made a brief movement with one hand to still her progress. A madman, obviously. The hand moved again, beckoning her forward.

"Do you see it?" the soft voice urged. "There—isn't it a beauty?"

Intrigued, Serena crouched down obediently. The butterfly hovered, wings extended in transparent brilliance for a timeless moment, then lifted gracefully into the air.

The young man rolled over and sat up, his arms resting casually on his knees. Piercingly intelligent blue-gray eyes surveyed her with lazy interest.

"Well, now," he said. "You must be my cousin Serena."

Mama would have said it was rude to stare so, but she could not for the life of her do otherwise. He was so much the opposite of all her imaginings.

He grinned suddenly and stood up, wiped his hand unhurriedly on the seat of his buff pantaloons, and held it out to her.

"I'm Cornwell. How do you do?"

She put hers into it and found it firmly grasped. The pale mobile face, which ill-health had pared into hollows, was made less severe by a well-shaped mouth, curved now into a smile of pure amusement.

"Well, there's a thing! You must outstrip me by all of two inches. Shall you mind, do you think? Has Mama bullied you into marrying me yet?" The questions were fired in quick succession, a good-natured barrage that left her breathless and laughing. The smile became a boyish grin. "That's much better."

"Oh, dear—and I had been imagining . . ." she halted, remembering some of her more lurid imaginings, and flushed in some confusion. "You are not at all what I expected."

Chapter Four

So, what *did* you expect—a gibbering idiot?"
"No, of course not!" But Serena could feel the
guilty color flooding her cheeks.

"Methinks the lady doth protest too much," he mocked
gently. "Not that I'd be surprised if you did expect the
worst. Stands to reason—a man who allows his mother
arrange his life without so much as a squeak of protest
don't exactly cut a romantic figure."

His description came so close to her own thoughts that
she instinctively bit her lip. Then, meeting his wry lopsided
smile, she found herself returning it.

"So, why did you?" she asked.

"Allow Mama full rein?" He appeared to be considering
the question. "I have no idea. I suppose I am too lazy to
argue with her—so fatiguing, don't you know."

"That I don't believe."

"You've obviously never tried to restrain my redoubtable
parent once she's taken the bit."

A fleeting vision of the duchess as a mare in full gallop
instantly reduced Serena to stifled mirth. "I can see it
wouldn't be the easiest task in the world."

She was feeling more at ease in her cousin's company
with every moment that passed and was thus emboldened
to probe further.

"Is your constitution really so delicate?"

"Oh, decidedly so. I have had it impressed upon me from infancy. It would appear that I was born prematurely—and having been dragged back from the brink no less than three times in my earliest years by a positive barrage of doctors and nurses, they realized that I was stubbornly determined to cling to life, and have continued so, in spite of having succumbed to every childhood disease known to man."

It was lightly said, but Serena's keen ear picked up an underlying note of frustration. How dreadful it must have been, to be forever ill, and to be watched over with such assiduous care. She thought of Harry and Edward, both so full of life, and wondered how they would have felt if they had been obliged to suffer a similar fate.

"It can't have been much fun."

"No. To compound my chapter of ills, an attack of rheumatic fever when I was five almost did for me. Seemingly, it damaged my heart, but by then I was so expert at cheating the grim reaper that he decided to let me live, so long as I confined myself to genteel pastimes." The lopsided smile was noticeably self-deprecating, his voice a trifle flat. "Hence my interest in butterflies. They are a fascinating breed—I have written a whole treatise on them. You must come and view my collection sometime."

A discreet cough made them turn, to see a portly middle-aged gentleman's gentleman endeavoring to attract his master's attention.

"Yes, Grove?"

"Her Grace desired me to inform Your Grace that tea will be taken shortly with your guests in the crimson drawing room." The valet cast a pained glance upon the streak of dirt marring the pale buff pantaloons. "I have taken the liberty of laying out a change of nether garments, knowing Her Grace's particularity in such matters."

"You spoil me, Grove."

"I do but perform my duty, Your Grace."

"So you do." The duke sighed. "How foolish of me. Very well. I will come directly."

The valet's gaze rested momentarily on Serena, his air of hauteur more marked. "Her Grace also intimated that if I should come upon Miss Fairburn, I was to inform her that Mrs. Fairburn has retired to her bedchamber to rest and refresh herself. Her Grace further intimated that, in the event of my coming upon the young lady, I should ascertain whether she wished me to escort her to her room."

Serena, irked by the valet's implied reproof, stammered, "How kind of Her Grace. Yes indeed . . . thank you. I will come at once. I had not meant to stray so far, or be away so long."

She was further embarrassed by the duke's wildly quirked eyebrow and the dawning realization that, used as she was to having brothers, she had been lulled by the duke's easy manner into treating him very much as she was used to treat them, and had thus allowed herself to become overfamiliar. He must be thinking her a veritable country cousin.

"Your Grace will excuse me?" she begged formally, determined to make amends.

"Not if you mean to poker-up on me like that," he said with mock displeasure. "You may call me Cousin, Coz, Cedric—even Cornwell if you must—but if you start *Your Grace-ing* me, I warn you I shall think very ill of you."

She laughed as relief overwhelmed her. "Your wish is my command, Cousin Cedric."

"That's much better." Irreverent humor lurked in his blue eyes. "Now, come along." He linked arms with her. "My good Grove, who looks after me so well, for all that he disapproves of my ramshackle ways, will direct you to your room where you may prepare yourself to face the tiresome but necessary ordeal by tea cups with Mama in the drawing room. To me, you look perfectly charming as you are, but take your time, and have no fear. Tea will wait upon you. And I shall be there to lend you moral support."

Somehow he made the prospect seem much less alarming, and it was with considerable confidence that she was able to encourage her mother, who was lying upon a huge boxlike bed, in an attempt to restore her nerves.

The room was overpoweringly gloomy and made the more so by a quantity of heavy furniture. Over in the darkest corner, Parkin, still pale from the journey, was laying out towels beside a gently steaming bowl of water on the washstand and muttering to herself about antiquated arrangements, quite unfitted for a lady as fastidious as her mistress.

Mrs. Fairburn looked very small and frail lying beneath the bed's looming canopy, but at the sight of her daughter she roused herself and stretched out a trembling hand.

"Oh, my dear child, there you are!" she cried faintly. "I had thought you lost forever. This place! I had quite forgotten how vast and oppressive it is. Quite medieval, in fact. And the duchess—so overbearing! I should not say this, I know, but I am convinced I could not be in her company above a day or two without succumbing to a severe bout of the megrims! Our situation surely cannot be so desperate as to . . . Oh, Serena, let us go home. Tomorrow! Truly, I should never have persuaded you to sacrifice yourself in this way . . ."

Serena sat beside her and took her hand in a comforting clasp. "Mama, don't take on so. You are just tired. To be sure, Masham is vast—I have been down I don't know how many corridors to get here, so that I began to wonder how we should ever find our way back to civilization." To her mother's surprise she smiled. "But I am reliably informed that someone will come to escort us."

"Well, indeed, I do hope you are right, but even so . . ." She looked more closely at Serena. "You look remarkably cheerful, I must say."

"Let us just say that things might not be quite so bad as we had supposed," she said with a provoking air of mystery. "I will tell you all about my little adventure as soon as I have made myself more presentable. I am only next door."

So it was that in the end, tea passed off rather better than had been expected. The duke set himself to charm Mrs. Fairburn, and she responded very much as a flower responds to water, thinking him a delightful young man. As for his being an invalid, no doubt the duchess, like most mothers, was overprotective, for aside from a hint of pallor, a certain languor in his manner, he seemed a perfectly normal young gentleman, possessed of pleasing looks and beautiful manners. Serena would go a long way to find a suitor half so fine. And he was exceedingly wealthy, to boot.

As Mrs. Fairburn prepared for dinner later that evening, her resolve to return home with all haste was quite forgotten, as she contemplated a future where the prospect of losing her daughter already seemed less of a sacrifice, and the benefits of such a union loomed large.

The duke was rich beyond her imaginings and had come of age, being rather more than six and twenty. To be sure, she would have liked him to display a little more resolution; his gentleness of disposition presently allowed his mother's influence to prevail more often than was proper, but with a good wife at his side, that influence would wane.

As for Masham Court itself, a little judicious refurbishing, the very fact of having more young life about the place, family visits—Serena would be sure to wish her family to visit often—and in time, a grandchild or two, their voices ringing through the gloomy corridors, and the house would take on quite a different aspect.

And for the family, it would mean an end to making do and all those tiresome tradesmen's bills, the boys' school fees need no longer present a problem, and her beautiful Emily—Mrs. Fairburn fell to air-dreaming. Serena, in her role as Duchess, would surely wish to give her sister a splendid come-out next year, even perhaps a presentation at Court, and escort her to lots of society balls, where Emily would undoubtedly attract the cream of the *ton*. Mrs. Fairburn saw no reason why she should not make every bit as good a marriage as her sister, for with her connections and her looks, she might surely look as high as she pleased!

Serena had expected her mama to moderate her dislike of Masham and all connected with it following her first meeting with Cousin Cedric, who was just the kind of young man she most liked, though even Serena had not looked for quite such a complete volte-face. She hardly knew whether to be amused or piqued by the speed with which Mama had changed her mind and decided that she must at least be thankful she had recovered her spirits.

Mrs. Fairburn could look remarkably pretty when she made the effort, and that evening, in her new black crepe, with her gray curls dressed up and adorned with a lace mantilla over a Spanish comb, she combined frailness with elegance in a way that made the duchess look at her a second time.

Serena, for so long resigned to cutting a relatively plain figure in her violet sarcenet, was unaware that the candlelight was particularly kind to her that evening, and that the color of her gown was warmly echoed in her eyes. There

was only one awkward moment as they were about to go
into dinner.

"Why, Serena, dear, you are not wearing your pearls,"
Mrs. Fairburn exclaimed. "They always look so pretty with
that gown. Do pray send someone to fetch them. I'm sure
Parkin will have no trouble laying her hands on them."

"Would you like me to go?" Miss Pennyweather, gentle
and vague, fluttered from the shadows, draped in her usual
array of scarves.

There was an awkward moment, and the duke's deceptively sleepy eyes saw the faint start, a glint of white as his
cousin's teeth closed on her lower lip before she said
lightly, "You are very kind, Miss Pennyweather, but I fear
you would have a wasted journey, for the truth is that in all
the hustle, I forgot to pack them."

"Oh, how vexatious!" Mrs. Fairburn turned to the
duchess. "Such a lovely rope of pearls—my late mama left
them to Serena."

"I do not in general care to see jewelry on very young
gels," boomed the duchess. "Though pearls must be considered quite unexceptionable."

"Oh, I do so agree."

Later, the ladies repaired to a smaller and rather more elegant salon fashioned in shades of yellow and green, leading off the dining room, leaving the duke in splendid
isolation to enjoy his port. Miss Pennyweather, primed by
the duchess, discreetly retired to her own quarters.

"Well now, Mrs. Fairburn," said the duchess, settling
herself in her own chair beside the fireplace and waving her
guests toward an adjoining brocaded sofa. "My son will be
with us soon, and I would very much like to be in a position
to present him with my decision. I have to tell you that,
having observed your daughter's behavior before and dur-

ing dinner, I have not been displeased. She conducts herself with a very proper modesty and decorum."

"I hope all my children know how to conduct themselves in company, ma'am," Mrs. Fairburn returned with an asperity that caused the duchess to raise her eyebrows and took her daughter by surprise.

Serena's own indignation swiftly turned to affection as her fingers closed reassuringly on her mother's clenched hand.

"Naturally. It is no less than I would expect," the dowager continued, impervious to the quiver in her guest's voice. "My ability to assess a character is acknowledged far and wide, and I am seldom proved wrong. There is perhaps a tendency in Miss Fairburn to put herself forward rather more than can be thought becoming in one so young, but I daresay that derives from being the eldest girl in a large family. Also, your own health being less than strong, she will have been used to take the lead—an admirable trait in many ways, though too much forwardness should be curbed."

Serena opened her mouth to speak, but was not given the opportunity to do so as the imperious stare was turned upon her. "You will be happy to know, however, that in general I am of the opinion that you and my son will suit."

Serena's indignation would no longer be quashed. She exclaimed impulsively, "But surely that is for him—for us—to decide."

The autocratic eyebrows shot up at the very idea that she should make so bold as to express an opinion, let alone take decisions on such momentous matters. "A very odd notion, to be sure. Naturally, the decision will be Cedric's, but I hope I know my son well enough to know that he will, as ever, be guided by me."

"And what is it that Cedric is to be called upon to decide—with your guidance—Mama?" queried the gentle voice.

The duke had entered unnoticed and stood just inside the door, a neat elegant figure in black knee breeches, brocade waistcoat, and a cutaway coat of wine-colored broadcloth, his cravat neat but not extravagant. A faint smile hovered about his lips though it did not reach his eyes, which were serious, even a trifle severe.

The duchess was momentarily discomposed, but swiftly recovered. "Pray, do not be tiresome, Cedric. You know very well that Mrs. Fairburn and her daughter were invited here for a specific purpose. And since I am satisfied that Colonel Fairburn's daughter will, with a little guidance from me, make you a proper wife, I have to tell you now that I am prepared to give my blessing to a betrothal between you and Miss Fairburn."

For a moment no one spoke. Then the duke said quietly, "And what does Miss Fairburn say to that?" He turned to Serena, who had risen to her feet in a state of agitation.

"If she has a modicum of sense, she will thank heaven to be accorded such an honor," exclaimed his mother, incensed.

"Miss Fairburn?" the duke persisted. There was a faint query in his eyes, which were still perfectly serious. "Let me first tell you that I would consider it an honor, were you to consent to be my wife, but I beg you will not feel yourself constrained to accept if you should not like the idea. We can always arrange matters another way," he concluded, ignoring a gasp of indignation from his mother.

Serena's indignation fell away when faced with his obvious concern. She smiled shyly. "You are very kind, Cousin, but indeed it is you who do me the honor, for to be sure we hardly know each other. However, if you are of the opinion that we should suit, I would do my best to be a good wife."

"Oh, my dear," murmured her mother, rising to clasp her daughter to her bosom. "So affecting! Such magnanimity on His Grace's part . . . I am sure you will be very happy. I could not wish for better . . ."

"So, the matter is settled," said the duchess tartly. "Though why you had to make such a piece of work of it all, my boy, when I had already arranged matters very satisfactorily, I cannot imagine."

"Nor I, Mama," he murmured in gentle self-mockery, "But perhaps it is time I began to assert myself. How else shall I ever bring myself to manage without you."

"Nonsense. Of course you will do so, given time," she acknowledged, quite oblivious of any irony. "But you need have no fear that I have any immediate plans to desert you. Instructions have already been given for a set of apartments to be prepared for me in the west wing. That way I shall still be close at hand to advise you and see that you do not overtax your strength."

Serena's heart sank, and she dare not look at her cousin. But fortunately, the arrival of the tea tray caused a slight hiatus. Miss Pennyweather being absent, the Duchess turned to Serena.

"Perhaps you would care to dispense tea, Miss Fairburn?" she said and watched with grudging approval as the younger woman handled the cups with deft fingers that trembled only slightly. "As to the marriage, there arises the question of your family being in black gloves," the complacent voice continued. "However, the problem is not insurmountable. A quiet family wedding in our own private chapel, presided over by our curate, Mr. Prost, will answer quite adequately. Any suggestion of pomp or celebration would be quite inappropriate in the circumstances and would in any case put too great a strain on Cedric's health. So, shall we say about two months from now?"

Serena, feeling that everything was rushing out of control, almost dropped the tea kettle, and in saving it, rattled the tray. "So soon?"

The duchess frowned. "We are agreed in principle. I see no reason to delay."

"Mama, you go too fast," Cedric interposed, seeing the confusion such haste would create, and aware that his cousin was about to say something extremely unwise. "Serena and I scarcely know each other."

"What has that to say to anything, I should like to know. I did not meet your father above twice before we married, but I knew what was expected of me. It is a matter of duty."

"Duty?" He almost spat the word out, causing his mother to draw herself up with awesome authority, prepared to deliver yet another lecture.

But it was Mrs. Fairburn, thrown into confusion by the prospect of losing her daughter and her prop far sooner than she had envisaged, who created the greater diversion. The room suddenly seemed very hot, almost unbearably so. "Oh, but Serena cannot possibly . . . I need . . . that is . . . she will need time . . ."

And again, it was Cedric, seeing her distress, who came to her rescue. "We all need time, Mama. Really, there is no need for such precipitate measures. I am hardly on my deathbed . . ."

"Cedric! I will not have you say such things!"

"Well, it is true. I cannot answer for Serena, but I for one, refuse to be rushed into marriage in such a hole-and-corner fashion. Nor will I be privy to tearing Serena willy-nilly from the bosom of her family, thus depriving Mrs. Fairburn of the support of her daughter so soon after their tragic loss."

The duchess marked the stubborn set of his chin. "My dear Cedric, what an unfeeling creature you must think me.

Oh, very well. Shall we say December, Mrs. Fairburn? A Christmas wedding. Four months should be long enough for anyone."

She took the muffled sound for assent and swept on. "Meanwhile, Miss Fairburn has much to learn in order to fit her to become mistress of Masham. Naturally, she will wish to return home in order to set certain preparations in train, though a large trousseau will not be necessary. Her needs can be better catered for here at Masham where I may supervise them."

It was becoming increasingly difficult for Serena to tolerate being spoken about as though she were not present. She was concentrating so hard on keeping her tongue between her teeth that she almost drew blood with the duchess's next pronouncement.

"Will three weeks suffice, do you suppose, Miss Fairburn?"

"I beg your pardon, ma'am? I did not quite . . ."

"Tch! I am proposing that you would benefit from a prolonged stay here beforehand, in order that you may familiarize yourself with all that being mistress of Masham entails. Would three weeks from now be convenient for you to take up residence?"

Three weeks! So short a time. And then she must leave forever all that was dearest to her. Serena glanced at her mother's stricken face, and a lump came to her throat. She bent her head, blinking fiercely in an attempt to master her feelings. Cedric's gentle voice came to her rescue.

"I believe a month would be more realistic."

The duchess shrugged. "Very well, Cedric. A month, though I cannot see what is so important that it must take so long. All the essential details may be attended to later." She turned to Serena. "A quiet wedding, then, as close to Christmas as may be convenient.

It was only a small reprieve, but Mrs. Fairburn welcomed the fact that she would have her daughter's support for a little longer. A tiny part of her was desolated that Serena would be denied the splendor of a grand society wedding. However, she was presently able to rouse herself to converse, if not with spirit, at least with a moderate degree of interest.

"Thank you," Serena said quietly when the duke presently drew her aside. "It is not that I wish to seem unwilling. Indeed, I am very conscious of the honor you do me. You have been very kind. But you must have observed how Mama is affected."

"She will miss you, I know. And you? How do you feel? Truly?"

"Apprehensive," she confessed.

He quirked an eyebrow. "Am I so terrifying?"

That drew from her a laugh. "No, indeed! Quite otherwise, in fact." They stood beside a pianoforte, and she began absently to leaf through the music without really seeing it. "But your mother is quite another matter."

"Rubbish. You must not allow her to bully you. From the little I already know of you, I suspect that you will soon be more than a match for Mama."

"I wish I could be sure of that. Everything is happening so quickly. Until a short time ago I was plain Serena Fairburn, living quietly with my family in modest seclusion, and with no pretensions to look higher . . ."

"I take exception to 'plain'," he said.

She blushed becomingly and said swiftly, "I have never minded about my appearance," and saw the eyebrow move again. "Well, only very occasionally."

"And now, suddenly, you are to become a duchess and will be obliged to put up with me and live in this great ugly barracks of a place."

"I doubt you will be difficult to live with," she said shyly. "As for the rest . . . Abby, our governess, always taught us that what can't be changed must be accepted with a good will."

"A wise woman, your governess."

"She is a dear. But I do worry about Mama. I have been used to fulfilling a great number of her duties, you see, especially since my father's death, and the family all look to me—Mama, the children . . ." She managed a faint rueful smile. "Emily has many excellent qualities, but she will not manage half so well, I think."

"I perfectly understand," he said sympathetically. "Emily is your sister?"

"Yes. She is sixteen and very pretty. But not at all practical."

"Ah." He allowed a small silence to elapse before saying diffidently, "On the subject of being practical, I hope you will not think me impertinent, Cousin, but did you really forget to bring your pearls?"

Taken by surprise, Serena looked quickly at him and away, but could not stop the guilty tide of color that betrayed her. "I really don't think that . . ."

"It's any of my business? Oh, you would be quite within your rights to tell me so. But as we are now, if as yet unofficially, betrothed, I may surely be permitted to show some concern?"

"If you must know"—pride was very evident in the sudden coolness of her voice, the lift of her chin—"there was some difficulty, a loan that my father had taken out. I daresay you can have no idea what it is like to be in difficulties over money . . ." She met his wry look and bit her lip. "Anyway, the matter was urgent, with other less pressing matters looming . . . In short, there seemed to be no way of settling it."

"So you sold your pearls?"

"Yes. Or, rather, our man of business, Mr. Price, has undertaken to sell them for me. Mama knows nothing of this, you understand?"

"Quite so. Well, from now on, your family's financial worries will be at an end." When she did not immediately reply, he glanced at her and saw the chin had taken a decided tilt. "That was not very tactful of me, was it?"

She looked up at him and smiled suddenly. "No, but then I am not a very gracious recipient, either. "Pride," as my governess, Miss Abbott, was used to quote at me, "goeth before destruction, and a haughty spirit before a fall.""

"Book of Proverbs, verses sixteen to eighteen," he returned promptly. "I would like to meet your Miss Abbott."

She laughed, and the atmosphere relaxed. "Oh, dear, I have crumpled this sheet of music beyond saving."

"It is not important," he said, taking it from her and discarding it. "From now on only one thing is important to me, dear cousin, your peace of mind."

"You are very kind."

The duke lifted her hand to his lips. "You are very easy to be kind to."

Mrs. Fairburn looked up in time to see this gallant gesture, and her bosom swelled with love and pride.

"Only look at them," she whispered to the duchess, quite forgetting the awe in which she held her.

The duchess, raising her pince-nez, seemed singularly unimpressed. "Are you at all musical, Miss Fairburn? I believe every gel should be proficient in some instrument. It is, if nothing else, a discipline."

"Oh, I do agree," Mrs. Fairburn hastened to say. "All my children are musically inclined. Serena plays the pianoforte quite beautifully and has—I venture to think—a more than passable singing voice."

Serena looked up to see her cousin solemnly wink at her, and she was hard put not to giggle.

"Perhaps Miss Fairburn will be so kind as to play something for us now," he said. "If there is any music to your taste, I will happily turn the pages for you."

As they bent over the music, she whispered, "How could you be so disobliging?"

"What about 'Cherry Ripe'?" he suggested blandly. "Or would something classical be more to your taste, perhaps?"

"I think not. 'Cherry Ripe' will do as well as any, I suppose." She sat down and struck the opening chord.

"That was quite pleasant," said Her Grace condescendingly when she had finished. "A light voice, but well enough."

Serena stood up. "You are more kind than I deserve, Your Grace," she said politely. "Now, if you would not mind," she added, "I believe that Mama is rather tired. If you have no objection, I believe she would like to retire."

"Is that so?" The duchess lifted her pince-nez as Mrs. Fairburn protested. "You do indeed look a trifle down-pin, ma'am. Very well. I suppose we can leave any further discussion about your daughter's future until tomorrow."

That night Serena's thoughts and feelings were in a tangle. Cedric was an agreeable young man, and she ought to thank heaven, for it might so easily have been otherwise. But everything was happening so quickly—too quickly.

As she drifted restlessly between sleeping and waking, the room seemed to be full of dark unfriendly shadows, accentuated by a three-quarter moon that shone almost directly into her eyes through a gap in the curtains, distorting the bulky furniture into sinister shapes the occasional creaking of the ancient beams and floorboards did nothing to soothe her nerves.

At last she rose, wrapped her dressing robe closely about

her, slid her feet into her slippers, and padded across to the window. The park lands stretched for miles, bathed in the cold silver light of the moon, and in the black sky a million stars glittered like chips of ice. It was very beautiful, awesome, in its almost unnatural stillness.

Serena was about to close the gap in the curtains when a pair of horses broke from the long dark shadow of the trees, moving with swift silent grace across the open fields away from the house, the foremost rider bent low across the horse's neck.

There was something very beautiful, yet vaguely sinister in the presence of the riders. She had no idea of the time, but it was late, too late, surely, for anyone from Masham to be about any ordinary business. She shivered and drew the curtain.

Chapter Five

Time was slipping away all too fast. Serena had tried to prepare the young ones for the time when she would no longer be there, and promised they should visit her very soon.

But this did not satisfy Mary. She wasn't sure what a duchess was, but protested tearfully that if it meant Serena going away forever, she didn't want her to be one.

"Baby!" Edward scoffed. "I can't wait. If Masham is as big and ancient as Serena says, it must have at least one ghost—more likely a dozen, I should think"—he lifted his arms dramatically—"floating round in big white sheets and rattling their chains! O-oooh!"

"Edward. Stop it at once!" Serena and Miss Abbey spoke together. But the damage was done. Mary would not be consoled, and Edward was banished to his room without his tea.

"Oh, dear," Serena sighed, laying aside her sewing.

"You mustn't worry," said Miss Abbey firmly as they sat by the nursery window in the afternoon sun. "Everything will work out splendidly. From all you have told me, nothing but good can come of your marrying the duke. He sounds charming, and only think of all you will be able to do to help your brothers and sisters."

"Oh, I know you are right. It's just . . ."

"That like all young women, you had secret air-dreams of being swept off your feet by some tall, dark, and devastatingly handsome stranger?"

Serena laughed, though just for an instant an image was conjured up unbidden of swirling capes and dark dangerous features. She blushed at the absurdity of her imaginings. She could never wish to be courted by such an ill-mannered man.

"Oh, I leave all that sort of thing to Emily," she said lightly. "I am too much of a beanpole to attract such a paragon, even if such a man exists, which I doubt."

The betraying blush did not escape Miss Abbey's notice. She was intrigued, but wisely did not press the matter. "Nonsense. You have many admirable qualities."

Serena wrinkled her nose. "Perhaps, but they are for the most part practical—not at all the kind to incite gentlemen to flights of love. In general, I fear I am more Rosalind than Celia."

"Well, we shall see." The governess thought it prudent to change the subject. "That is going to be a very pretty gown, my dear. Your favorite color."

"It *is* rather beautiful." Serena lifted the rich lavender-gray silk, letting its softness ripple through her fingers. The material had been expensive, but Mama had been insistent that she must consider her future status.

"You will be expected to dress well, my dear. And since *Dear Cedric* has been so generous in his settlement, we must not let him down. I do not perfectly understand it all, but Mr. Price assures me that I need have no financial worries ever again!"

The sigh of relief that accompanied this last had obliged Serena to hide a smile, for over the years her mama had never, to her knowledge, troubled her head unduly about such matters, being convinced that she had but to confide her problem to Mr. Price, senior—and all would be well. To give him due credit, though she sometimes wondered how he managed it, all usually had been well.

From choice Serena would have preferred so generous a settlement to be deferred until after her marriage, but Cedric had been surprisingly adamant, pointing out that her mother's security and peace of mind must outweigh any scruples she might have in the matter. And so she had agreed. The money had come too late, however, to save her pearls. They had been sold for a handsome price—an anniversary present for a gentleman's wife—only a day or two before she had returned home.

"It is a little frustrating to be so confined." She sighed and applied her needle once more to the lavender gown. "But I could not belittle Pa's memory by venturing so soon into bright colors."

Abby was about to speak when they heard the sound of wheels on gravel, followed a moment later by a great bustling below and a familiar cheerful voice upraised.

"I'm sure—yes, it's Harry!" Serena exclaimed, laying aside her work and hurrying to the door. "We didn't expect him for another two days! I do hope he is not sent home in disgrace again."

There were feet on the stairs, a cheerful voice upraised, and there he was, his coat crumpled and already straining at the shoulders, although it was new not three months ago, his fair hair disheveled. Brother and sister embraced, and then Serena held him away.

"Dear boy, how is this? We didn't look for you so soon! Heavens, you must have grown at least three inches!"

"It's all right, Sis. I haven't done anything dreadful this time." He grinned. "Some of the first years went down with measles, so they sent us all packing before the infection spread."

"Well, I hope you haven't brought it home with you," Serena said, her joy at seeing him tempered with the possibility of passing any infection on the young ones, to say nothing of the duke.

"Silly!" he chided her. "I had it when I was eight, remember?"

"So you did. Have you seen Mama yet? She will be overjoyed to have you home."

And at least, she thought, the family will be almost complete, if only for a few more days.

Cedric had formed the intention of traveling to Mountford himself to escort Serena back to Masham, rejecting as absurd his mother's fears that the two-way journey would put an unnecessary strain on his fragile health.

"It is not much above forty miles, Mama. If Mrs. Fairburn can attempt such a journey, I can certainly do so."

"A silly woman," scoffed the duchess. "Her megrims are self-induced. She does not, I venture to suggest, suffer as you do from any chronic weakness of the heart—or indeed any other comparable disability."

Cedric felt frustration welling up in him, but his innate good manners triumphed, so that his voice was only a trifle cool as he persisted, "Perhaps not. But not everyone is as indomitable as you, Mama." He had not intended this as a compliment, though she clearly took it to be one. He said in more conciliatory tones, "I am not quite helpless, you know, and Mrs. Fairburn has very kindly invited me to stay for a few days, so I shall be well rested for the return journey."

No more had been said on the matter, though he was obliged to endure several very uncomfortable silences that spoke volumes. However, such was his relief when the moment arrived for him to depart, that he was able to take his leave of Her Grace with genuine affection, accepting her strictures meekly in the knowledge that glorious freedom beckoned.

"I am surprised that Grove did not insist upon your wearing a topcoat," she declared, accompanying him to the West Front where the traveling coach waited, and eyeing his buff breeches, top boots, and olive green coat with disapproval. "It would never do if you were to take a chill."

"I shan't, Mama," he assured her with a smile. "The sky is as clear and blue as one could wish for, the prelude to a perfect late summer's day, in fact—exactly right for going a'courting."

Her Grace was not normally prey to uncertainty. But just for a moment she found herself torn between mother love and a quite genuine fear for his health—and, worse, a more insidious fear that little by little he was growing away from her, beginning to resist her influence. It irked her to reflect that she might have been mistaken in fostering this idea of a betrothal, for she prided herself on her good judgment. Only a fierce determination to keep the control of the estate effectively in her hands had persuaded her that in order to secure her hold on the reins, Cedric must marry and produce an heir, a grandson, whom she and she alone would guide and direct in the right and proper paths. "Well, get along with you then. And be sure to send word that you have arrived."

Imposing as she was in her black crepe morning gown, with a sable-lined cloak thrown about her shoulders and a turban of statuesque proportions crowning her graying hair, she nonetheless looked momentarily vulnerable, causing Cedric to lean forward and kiss her cheek with sudden affection.

"Tch! Such a fuss!" she exclaimed, holding her head very high as she watched his retreating figure.

He smiled, checked the urge to run lightly down the steps, and instead walked decorously to the waiting coach, feeling only the slightest bit guilty at deceiving her, for, unbeknown to his mother, he had sent Robbie Gibson, his groom, ahead of the traveling coach to the first change with his much loved gelding, Starlight, so that he might relieve the boredom of the journey by riding part of the way.

It was a move deplored by Grove, who in a mood of silent disapproval had packed a whole case full of James' Powders and other physics, potions, and medicaments in anticipation of the outcome of such rash behavior. And when later, after an hour or so in the saddle, his young master seemed to experience nothing worse than a slight shortness of breath, far from being reassured, Grove hinted darkly that time would tell.

Cedric handed Starlight over to Robbie and resumed his seat in the coach. He leaned back and closed his eyes against a sudden dizziness, making a conscious effort to subdue the wheezing breath that threatened to betray him as he waited for his heart to assume a more regular beat. He was more fatigued than he would admit.

All his life he had been pursued by physicians, relations, and friends, each of whom in one way or another seemed determined to stifle any attempt to exert himself, however harmless the pastime—the only exception being his cousin, Darcy, who scoffed at his supposed weakness and had introduced him to the subtle art of subterfuge. Without Darcy he would not have learned to ride, to shoot—though never for sport—or to become proficient in games of chance.

The two former, once discovered, were actively discouraged by the family doctor as putting a severe strain upon his heart, that most delicate of organs, though a little gentle riding with a groom always close at hand had been permitted when it became obvious that to deny him this small pleasure might do more harm than good. And Cedric had taken good care that any deviation from this routine remained known only to Darcy.

The gentle walks prescribed for him years ago by Dr. Handly, taken in the company of his curate, Mr. Prost, had been unexpectedly redeemed from total boredom by the reverend gentleman's interest in flora and fauna, as a result of which Cedric had discovered in himself a hitherto unexplored talent for painting nature's smallest creatures in all their exquisite detail.

He had by now completed several volumes of paintings, each devoted to a particular species, together with careful observations of their habitat, lifetime, etc. His mother thought his hobby curious, even a little unmanly, though she became very defensive when Darcy teased him about it. At least, she observed caustically, it kept him occupied.

Cedric was aware that the question of the succession—and the alternative, the breaking up of the estate—had vexed her mind for a considerable time. For his part, he was quite happy to go on as he was, and thought it a great pity that Darcy wasn't in line to succeed. A dukedom would sit much more easily on his cousin's shoulders. But when he was so misguided as to propound these views to his mother, his complacence had aroused her indignation.

"Lynton, indeed! Oh, he's well enough in his way—charm the birds off the trees if he's a mind to—charmed your father into including him in his will. But a fine thing it would be an' a shameless rakehell like Lynton should ever be permitted to fill Masham with his light-o-loves!"

This prospect had so titillated Cedric's imagination that he was obliged to excuse himself and leave the drawing room before mirth overcame him.

He was less amused when he realized that his remarks had brought home to his mama the full horror of what the

future might hold for her, should anything happen to him.
The title would die out and she would be obliged to share
the estate with her husband's relations—a feckless family,
of whom Darcy was the only tolerable member.

Thus Cedric's levity had inadvertently set in train a series of tiresome examinations as doctors were summoned
and consulted as to the possibility of his being able to
marry and produce an heir without seriously endangering
his life.

After much head shaking they decided that, with reason-
able care, and the right wife, his constitution should with-
stand the rigours of married life. And, when apprised of the
verdict, he accepted it as he had long since learned to accept the inevitable—with a good grace.

In the event, however, his cousin, Serena, had come as a
pleasant surprise. During her brief stay she had never once
made him feel like an invalid, so if he must marry, he could
only thank heaven that for once his mama had chosen well.

"He's here! He's here!" Edward cried, clambering down
from the window seat in the nursery, where he and Mary
had spent most of the afternoon with their noses pressed
against the glass, Miss Abbott having abandoned up all
hope of giving their thoughts a more studious direction.

From below came the sound of wheels crunching on the
gravel drive, but as Edward bolted for the door, Miss Abbott's hand was there to stem his headlong rush, her voice
calm but firm.

"We will have none of that, if you please. Whatever will
His Grace think, faced with such a skimble-skamble pair.
Your mama and Serena will need time alone with the duke,
which will give you and Mary plenty of time to go and
wash your face and hands. And you can then change into
your best nankeen suit . . . ."

"Oh, must I?" he wailed.

"Yes, you must. You want to make a good impression, don't you?"

Edward wasn't at all sure that he did, but the steely glint in Abby's eyes prohibited argument.

"Mary, I think a change of pinafore will suffice for you." The little girl's mouth trembled. "That isn't fair! If Teddy is to wear his best, I want my pink muslin!"

"Very well. Just this once. And if you are good, I will tie your hair up with a ribbon."

Downstairs in the parlor, which had been polished until it shone, the ladies waited. Serena for once bore no resemblance to her name. For an hour past, she had been obliged to listen to her mother's nonstop discourse upon the necessity of making the duke's brief stay a pleasant one.

"I am very displeased that Harry is not back from the Bennetts," she said for the umpteenth time. "He promised me most faithfully that he would be here."

"I'm sure the duke will not take Harry's absence amiss, Mama," she said soothingly.

"But so much depends upon first impressions. I am still of the opinion that we should have made an effort to refurbish the parlor. When one remembers the elegance of the Masham salons . . ."

Emily, turning to exchange an amused glance with her sister, was surprised to catch Serena lifting a finger unobtrusively to smooth the place above her right eye which usually denoted that she had the headache. If I were about to welcome a duke as my betrothed, she thought, you wouldn't catch me succumbing to a headache.

And then the doorbell pealed. Mrs. Fairburn fell silent, footsteps were heard in the hall, and Ruby, wide-eyed and breathless, announced, as she had rehearsed over and over again, "His Grace, the Duke of Cornwell."

He came in swiftly as though anxious to get the ordeal over, his slight figure showing to advantage in a well-cut coat of blue superfine and neatly tied cravat, biscuit-colored pantaloons, and gleaming Hessian boots. He paused momentarily in the doorway, pale of face, and with an air of reserve about him that made Serena's heart sink.

However, "You are most welcome, Your Grace," she said, rising to greet him, and his gentle smile immediately set her foolish fears at rest.

His relief at finding her just as he had remembered her was as great as hers. He took her hand and raised it to his lips. Its faint tremor surprised him, and in a curious way gave him added confidence.

"So formal, Coz?" he quizzed her. "Never tell me that you, too, have been feeling ridiculously nervous? Now that I am here I cannot think why I was so foolish."

He crossed to where Mrs. Fairburn sat in her fireside chair, her cheeks pink with pleasure at the compliment.

"Ma-am," he said, bowing over her hand. "It is indeed a great pleasure to meet you again so soon. I hope you are in better health, and that your kindness in letting me stay will not inconvenience you."

She again coloured with pleasure, and murmured something incoherent to the effect that she was very happy to welcome him to their humble abode.

"Oh, never say humble, ma'am. Your home is quite charming," he said gallantly. "A true home, in fact. I dare swear it is not plagued by one single draughty corridor."

"I sincerely hope not." Serena laughed, suddenly feeling completely at ease. "Cousin Cedric, may I present my sister, Emily?"

Emily dipped a curtsy, and he handed her up with solemn grace. "Serena told me you were very beautiful. I see she did not exaggerate."

Emily's cerulean eyes smiled up at him from under their long lashes. He was not at all her idea of a duke, for he had none of Lord Lynton's dash and style. But he had very pleasant manners and a quiet charm.

Ruby had already informed everyone below stairs that the young duke, for all that he was a bit on the delicate side, was all that a young lady might look for, with lovely manners—not a bit puffed up like that other one. In fact, she reckoned that Miss Serena could count herself the luckiest young lady in the world.

Cedric even found favor with the children, though Edward had at first stared very hard at him before blurting out, "Are you really a duke?"

His Grace lifted a quizzical eyebrow. "So I have always been led to believe."

"You don't look like a duke," Edward persisted.

"Edward!" Mrs. Fairburn shot up in her chair, with visions of her daughter's betrothal foundering at the outset on the obstacle of her son's insensitivity.

But Cedric held up a hand. "Pray let the boy speak, ma'am. 'Out of the mouths of babes' an' all that." He addressed Edward with suitable gravity. "I can quite see that I must be a sad disappointment to you, but I never had a role model, d'you see. My father died when I was young—younger than you. So, I would be very much in your debt if you could give me a pointer or two. How do you suppose a duke *should* look?"

Edward frowned, taking this responsibility thrust upon him very seriously. "I'm not precisely sure, sir . . . sort of large and red-faced, and important, I suppose."

"Ah! Well . . . that does make things rather difficult. I doubt there is much chance that I shall grow any more, d'you see."

In an effort to be helpful, Edward added, "P'raps if you

had a coat with lots of capes, and an eyeglass . . . Lord Lynton called a few weeks ago, and he looked like a regular lord."

"Teddy!" Serena was mortified. "Do try to think before you speak!"

"I *am* thinking! He asked me . . ."

I did, indeed," said the duke, taking it like a man. "So, Darcy has been here, stealing my thunder, has he? Ah, well, he's certainly a splendid fellow. I can quite see that I must be a sad disappointment by comparison."

"I'm not disappointed, 'xactly," the boy hastened to explain with ingenuous candor. "He was very grand and proud, but I think you are probably much nicer."

"Thank you, Edward," Cedric murmured. "You have quiet restored my bruised ego."

Edward wasn't sure what a bruised ego was, but the duke seemed quite pleased, so he magnanimously offered to take him up to the nursery to show him his paintings.

However, Serena had been studying her cousin under cover of the conversation and saw that, despite his efforts to rise to the occasion, he could not quite conceal the weariness in his eyes, or his pallor, and there was a hint of blue about his lips.

"Not now, Teddy," she said firmly. "You have entertained His Grace enough for one day. I'm sure he would like to go to his room to rest for a while. There will be time enough tomorrow to show him all your treasures."

The duke demurred, but there was a fleeting gleam of relief in his eyes as she insisted. At that moment the door flew open and Harry entered in his usual rush.

"Sorry, the time went so fast. I would have been here sooner, only Freddie had the most splendid kite, and it got stuck up a tree—oh, I say!" He stopped, seeing that their grand visitor had arrived.

"Harry, you are the limit!" Serena exclaimed, eyeing his crumpled appearance. "Cedric, this disreputable young wretch is my brother Harry."

Harry bit his lip ruefully as Cedric extended his hand in greeting. "If you'll excuse me, sir, I think I'd best not . . ." He held his own uppermost to show the palm all streaked with dirt. "I had to climb up the tree, you see, to rescue the kite, and the branches were all covered with moss . . ."

"Ah, yes." The duke smiled. "I perfectly understand."

Mrs. Fairburn, fearing that this lack of respect might bring all her dreams tumbling down, uttered a faint cry and pressed a handkerchief to her lips.

Serena was merely mortified. "Harry, how could you? You haven't been home five minutes, and I told you most particularly—"

"It's all right, Serena," Cedric interposed swiftly, with his lopsided smile. "I envy Harry. I'm sure it is perfectly natural, at his age, for kites to take preference over mere dukes."

Harry, who was almost as tall as the duke, grinned back at him. "Thanks, sir. You're a real prime 'un."

"An accolade, indeed," Cedric murmured when Serena presently showed him to his room.

She laughed. "I suspect you have made a friend for life, but I could cheerfully have strangled him, though by now I should be used to young brothers. We dine at seven, by the way," she said, noticing how his breath became a trifle labored as they climbed the stairs. "But if you would prefer to rest—have something on a tray in your room . . ."

He paused and turned to look at her. "Serena, I am constantly surrounded by people who cosset me, for my own good, of course," he said wearily. "I had hoped that you, at least, would not treat me so shabbily."

"I don't mean to, truly. But you have had a long and tiring journey."

"And shall recover after a short rest. I do know my limits, and I promise you, I am not quite the poor delicate creature my dear mama would have everyone believe."

"It must be very trying for you to have your every move
watched over." She half-smiled and bit her lip. "I'll try to
remember not to do so if you will promise not to let Edward pester you. He can be very persistent."

"I won't. But you see, I have never until now experi-
enced the enthusiasm of young company, and I find it most
refreshing."

"Well, if you're sure." She smiled. "Just don't hesitate to
stop him when you've had enough. He is remarkably re-
silient and will bear you no malice."

As Serena handed the duke over to Grove, and the door
closed behind them, she could not help but linger to hear
the valet's rough concern as he fussed over his charge like
a mother hen.

"There now, Your Grace. Didn't I say as you would
knock yourself up with all that jauntering about? What Her
Grace would have to say about it, I don't know, I'm sure.
It'll be bellows-to-mend with Your Grace if you carry on at
this rate."

"Don't fuss, Grove. I shall be fine directly."

"There I must beg leave to differ, Your Grace. A nice
lie-down is what's needed—if we can just have that coat
off, and your Hessians—that's the ticket. I have your
physic all ready. It needs but a word to Miss Fairburn, and I
vow she will arrange for a light repast to be served to you
here . . ."

Serena hovered uncertainly, wondering whether she
ought to have pressed the matter harder when Cedric's ex-
asperated voice stayed her hand.

"Enough, man! An hour's peace and quiet will serve me better than your precious laudanum. If you want to make yourself useful, you may lay out my evening clothes, for when I am fully rested, I have every intention of dining with the family."

Chapter Six

The following day dawned misty, giving way to sunshine before the family had finished breakfast.

Much to Serena's relief, the duke had agreed without argument to have breakfast in his room.

"I'm sure you would prefer it," she told him. "And I am not cosseting you. It is simply that the children are bursting with energy first thing in the morning. When Connaught is home, he refuses point blank to take his meals in their company."

In fact, the children almost always had their breakfast in the nursery, but she did not say so, absolving herself from misleading comment in the knowledge that her motives were pure. They also proved to have been entirely justified, for when Cedric did finally put in an appearance halfway through the morning, he looked much more rested and expressed a desire to take a walk if she should like it.

"I'll fetch my bonnet and shawl," she said, wishing that just for once she might be permitted to wear something light and more becoming. But at least the brown gown she wore most mornings was less depressing than unrelieved black.

They took the path that led from the front of the house in a sweeping curve toward the back, where it divided, the right fork leading to the stable buildings. Here they lingered briefly among the gleaming harness and tack and the single shabby gig that had been lovingly polished. Cedric was introduced to George, who had been with the family forever as groom and gardener.

"He should have been pensioned off years ago," Serena murmured as they approached, "but he still lives above the stable—the only home he knows—and likes to feel he is still of some use. A boy from the village occasionally helps him with the garden."

They found George polishing some of the little-used horse brasses. "No sense lettin' good tackle go to rack an' ruin, fer want of a bit of elbow grease, Y'r Grace. These young uns got no idea 'ow ter bring up a shine on a nice bit o' brass."

"Well, it does you credit, George, it does indeed," said the duke, his eye caught by signs of activity in the small paddock beyond where a lively bay filly was running rings round a much older pony, who flicked a contemptuous tail when she occasionally came too close.

"Yours?" he asked Serena.

"Not really, though I like to pretend she is. Connaught bought Firefly for Harry last time he was home. But at least I have the pleasure of exercising her while Harry is away at school."

"I didn't know you rode," Cedric said enthusiastically. "When we are married, you shall have as many horses as you wish."

She laughed. "What shocking extravagance! *One* would do very nicely."

"My own Starlight is presently stabled at the Swan in Mountford. If you have someone who could take a message, my groom will bring him over. Then we can ride out together."

"I'd like that," Serena said. "George will gladly go. He welcomes any excuse to slope off to the Swan."

They walked on, taking the other fork of the path round to the rear of the house, where an oval lawn was presently surrounded by a herbaceous border in its full riot of late summer colors and perfumes.

"Perfect for butterflies," he said with a smile, remembering how they had first met.

Serena laughed. "You gave me quite a shock. When first I saw you lying so still, I wasn't sure who you were or what you were—or whether you were ill or dead!"

The smile became a grin. "Or mad?" he suggested. "Confess now—you must have thought me very odd, a man obsessed by butterflies!"

"Only in those first moments, and you must allow that I was in a state of high indignation. Following upon my daunting interview with your mother, I was in exactly the right frame of mind to imagine the worst. You can have no idea how relieved I was when you spoke."

"Were you, truly?" Cedric turned her to face him and took her hands. "Serena, I would not have you unhappy for the world. Promise you will tell me if you find marriage to me repugnant?"

"But I don't!"

"Truly? I am not unaware of your circumstances and could always arrange matters so that your family did not suffer," he persisted.

High up in the apple tree a blackbird trilled its long, pure notes. For an instant the sound pierced her heart, puncturing forever any lingering romantic notions, for like most young girls she had dreamed her dreams. But such love was not for the likes of her. Cedric was a sensitive caring man who would always be kind and affectionate, and she liked him enormously.

"I am more fortunate than I deserve," she said softly. "If you are content, I must be doubly so."

"Oh, I am well content. It is probably too soon to give you a bride present, but I have one for you just the same." From the inner pocket of his coat he took a box she instantly recognized.

"My pearls! But how . . . ?"

"I can be surprisingly resourceful when necessary, and your story of the pearls touched me deeply. It seemed to me the sooner you had them back, the better. It wasn't difficult for my own man of business to trace your Mr. Price."

"He said a gentleman had bought them as an anniversary present for his wife," Serena exclaimed indignantly and blushed, remembering what he had paid for them.

"Well, that was not so far removed from the truth. A betrothal is a kind of anniversary, after all, and you will, before long, be my wife." Cedric drew her forward and kissed her mouth. His lips were firm and cool and lingered just a little longer than was necessary.

"Love's young dream—how very touching!" drawled a voice Serena remembered all too well.

"Darcy! By all that's famous!" Cedric released Serena with embarrassing haste and turned to see his cousin striding toward them, his coat billowing out behind him. "What brings you here?"

"Not 'what', young Ceddie—who," he returned carelessly. "I found myself in the vicinity of Masham and called to see how you went on, only to find you had flown the coop. Her Grace seemed to think you might be in need of my support, So I drove here, post haste, to see for myself." He looked from one rather pink face to the other. "But you seem to be managing very well without any help from me. Forgive me. I am clearly *de trop*."

"Don't be an ass!" Cedric exclaimed, pink with mingled

annoyance and embarrassment. "It really is too bad of Mama! As if I am not already surrounded by her minions, all bent on suffocating me with their care, without roping you in, too!"

"Oh, acquit me, dear boy," Lynton said carelessly. "I hope you know me better than to suppose that I wish to shield you from every wind that blows. If the truth be known, I came, thinking to rescue you."

"From what? Or should I say whom?"

"Why, from the very minions you complain of, Ceddie. Who else?" he said smoothly, and turning, removed his hat and made Serena the most elegant of legs, though his eyes mocked her. "Y're servant, ma'am."

"Oh, how remiss of me," Cedric said hurriedly. "Darcy, I must make my fiancée, Miss Fairburn, known to you." Cedric blushed a little, suddenly shy. "Serena, this is my cousin Darcy, the Earl of Lynton. He lives only a few miles from us, and I count him as one of my few real friends."

"Very prettily done, my boy. But Miss Fairburn and I are already acquainted. I suppose you might say it was I who brought you together, being the bearer of Her Grace's initial communication." The edge of sarcasm in his voice was unmistakable. "No need to ask how you do, Miss Fairburn. You are clearly in fine bloom—rather like your admirable garden. The prospect of ascending to the ranks of the peerage obviously holds no terrors for you. Quite the reverse, in fact."

Serena resented the mocking innuendo, as much for Cedric's sake as for her own, and that resentment lent an added edge to her anger, though for Cedric's sake she took refuge in levity.

"I am trying to hold my elation in check, my lord," she said and heard Cedric chuckle. She also noticed with some satisfaction that Lord Lynton's smile did not reach his eyes. "Did Ruby tell you where you might find us, my lord?"

"No. I was about to pull the bell when I heard voices and thought I recognized Ceddie's, so I took the liberty of coming in search of him. Jack is walking the horses—" He lifted an eyebrow. "You will remember Jack? In a sense, I suppose you could say I was guilty of trespass. If you should wish to have me thrown out . . ."

It was there again, that veiled mockery.

"I would not dare, my lord," she returned lightly.

She drew herself up to her full height, which usually gave her an advantage. But Lord Lynton still stood a good half a head taller, so that she was obliged to look up at him. To make bad worse, the sun was full in her eyes, forcing her to squint.

"Don't let Darcy vex you, Serena," Cedric said with a grin. "He can be an infuriating fellow—does it quite deliberately, y'know. But there's no real harm in him."

Serena wasn't at all sure about that. However, she made a supreme effort for her cousin's sake. "I am not in the least vexed," she said lightly. "Having grown up with three brothers, I am well up to such tricks. I have always believed that every girl should have at least one brother. A few years spent in the nursery, observing their posturing and petty tyrannies would teach them a great deal about the male ego—enough, I vow, to banish forever the myth that man is the superior sex."

"Oh-ho! What a facer!" Cedric chortled. "Dashed if I've ever heard anyone give you such a put-down, my brave cousin!"

"A palpable hit. But I shall come about." Lynton forced a smile, which again failed, quite, to reach his eyes. "You hold strong opinions, Miss Fairburn. Which makes me more than ever intrigued to know how it comes about that the duchess has consented to Ceddie's taking such a strong-minded female to wife?"

"I am not privy to Her Grace's inmost thoughts, and if I were, I hope I know when to speak and when to hold my tongue," she said demurely, quietly triumphant in the knowledge that she had at last succeeded in rattling him. "However, I am being a very poor hostess. Gentlemen, do come inside and allow me to offer you some refreshment."

"Thank you—a few moments only. The horses will grow restive if I stay too long."

Over Madeira and ratafia biscuits, the two young men discussed polite generalities in deference to Serena, and also to Emily, who had joined the party. Cedric, in the short time he had been with them, had brought out the best in Emily, and although Lynton was still her idea of a romantic hero, Serena was pleased she managed to converse without making a cake of herself—and thanked heaven that Harry was out with his friend.

The conversation eventually came round to the question of the return journey to Masham Court.

"When were you thinking of leaving, Ceddie?"

"We have not yet decided." The duke glanced at Serena. "I'm bound to say that I am enjoying myself prodigiously, and having slipped the leash, am in no hurry to return. However, it is for Serena to decide. I must not outstay my welcome."

"You could never do that," Serena put in quickly. "And I'm sure that a few days here would do you a world of good. Mama is happy for you to stay as long as you please. And I know everyone else would be equally happy, especially Teddy, who is looking forward to showing you his drawings."

Lynton's eyebrow quirked as he looked from one to the other. "How very domesticated. But surely Her Grace will be expecting you. Are not your rooms already reserved at the Crossed Keys for the return journey?"

"That's no problem," said the duke, reveling in his burgeoning sense of freedom. "I'll dispatch one of the postillions to cancel them. And while he's at it, he can take a letter to Mama, informing her of our revised plans."

"Egad! But I'd give a monkey to be there when she receives the news, my little bantam cock!" Lynton drawled softly.

"Stuff!" Cedric grinned, unoffended. "It's high time I asserted myself. I should have done it long ago."

"Famous last words. It's easy enough to be brave from a safe distance." His lordship rose to take his leave. "But do let me know when you mean to return to Masham, Ceddie, and I'll drive over to pick up the pieces."

Serena insisted on seeing him out. Pausing on the step, he looked down at her, the mockery gone in eyes suddenly grown hard.

"I daresay you think you have been very clever, Miss Fairburn. But we shall see."

Edward was out on the drive with Jack where the curricle waited. They seemed to have established an uneasy peace, with Jack instructing the younger boy in the finer points of handling such a bang-up rig. The sight of the two young boys reassured Serena, whose heart had been beating rather faster than was comfortable.

It was, in fact, a further week before His Grace reluctantly decided that he could no longer put off his return, by which time he had become very much a part of the family.

The leave-taking was not achieved without tears. Emily was almost offhand, which drew a reproachful rebuke from her mama, but Serena was not deceived. Emily's tears had all been noisily shed the previous evening in the privacy of their bedroom.

"I'm going to m-miss you so much!" she sobbed, and they had clung together, their tears mingling. "I'm not half so g-good with Mama as you . . . and there w-will be no one to talk to . . ."

Serena had smoothed back Emily's golden curls, smiling through her own tears. "That is nonsense, my dearest. You will have Jane—you are always saying that she is your best friend. And you will be able to come and stay at Masham once I am settled, though you may find it less comfortable than our own dear home."

She would have been more worried, had she not been certain Emily would very quickly adjust to life without her. She was less certain about Mama, who was suddenly looking very small and lost. Cedric had noticed this also and sought to reassure her.

"You may be sure, ma'am, that I shall take the greatest care of Serena," he told Mrs. Fairburn. "And I hope you will all come to visit us very soon."

"You are a dear, kind boy," she said, having quite lost her awe of him. She dabbed at her eyes with an already sodden and totally inadequate scrap of lawn handkerchief. "I shall miss my dear girl most dreadfully . . ." her voice trembled, "but I could not wish to see her more happily bestowed."

The baggage had been accommodated in a second, less elaborate coach where Grove had already taken his place, his lugubrious expression concealing a profound thankfulness that they would soon be back where they belonged. His pleasure marred only by the necessity of being obliged to share the journey with a young maidservant, by name, Bessie Figg, who was Cook's niece.

She was a likable, efficient girl, according to Miss Fairburn—though Grove reserved judgment, placing little faith in his master's bethrothed's ability to know what was what.

For the first few miles Serena sat with her hands tightly clasped in her lap, staring blindly out of the window, and Cedric, acutely sensitive to her mood, made no attempt to break the silence.

At last she turned to him. "I'm sorry. I'm not very good company, am I?"

He saw the tears drying on her cheeks and laid a long, slim hand over hers. "My dear, considering all things, I think you are being remarkably restrained. But we are no great distance away, and you may visit as often as you wish . . ."

"Oh, Cedric!" she exclaimed on a half sob. "How good you are to me! You will not regret it, I promise."

"Now you are being nonsensical, as well as pitching grossly wide of the mark, for I am by nature a selfish creature, as you will doubtless discover in time. In fact, had you elected to cry all down the front of my coat," he concluded in his droll way, "you might well have found my goodness stretched to the limit."

"Idiot!"

"Oh, that much I grant you." After a moment his tone changed and his eyes were suddenly serious. "Will you make me one small promise, Serena? Nothing that has happened thus far is irrevocable, and should you at any time wish to reconsider, promise that you will tell me, and we will find some other way."

"Thank you," she said huskily. "But I would be a great fool to change my mind."

"Nevertheless, I'd liefer there was honesty between us at all times." His fingers tightened for a moment, and then he released her.

The day, which had begun chilly, was now picking up,

and the sun broke through the clouds. They made excellent time, the duke's own grooms being ready at each posting inn with fresh horses as they skirted Salisbury Plain and stopped for a light luncheon at Steeple Langford.

"We should reach the outskirts of Salisbury before the light goes," the duke said. "I have bespoken rooms for the night at the Cross Keys. I hope you will find it tolerably comfortable."

"I'm sure I shall. I believe we stayed there last month when Mama and I came to visit."

"Very likely. The landlord, Purdy, is an excellent fellow. Always makes his best rooms available to us, no matter how short the notice."

He spoke casually, yet with the engaging certainty of one who had, as Mama was wont to say, "come into the world hosed and shod." Serena smiled to herself. It must be very strange to have one's every whim gratified. She was not altogether sure she would like it, or indeed, that it was necessarily a good thing to be so indulged, though perhaps, just for a while, it might be fun.

"How shockingly spoiled you are."

Her mockery was gentle and quite without malice. He returned her a whimsical smile.

"Am I? I daresay you are right. You will have to reform me."

As if to prove her point, the landlord was at the door to greet them before the coach had come to a halt, eager to usher them in.

"An honor to have you with us again so soon, Your Grace," he said with many a bow. "Your rooms are ready, if you and the young lady should be wishful to rest for a while?"

"Thank you. I am not tired. But perhaps Miss Fairburn would appreciate a rest?" He glanced at Serena.

She smiled. "No, indeed. Though I would like to wash—to refresh myself."

The landlord was all graciousness. "Of course. By all means. If you'll just come along to the private parlor, I shall send for Ruth to take you upstairs at once."

His glance, passing discreetly over Serena's plain black bonnet and cloak, betrayed not a hint of the curiosity that consumed him as he led them along the passage. A few flagons of ale in the taproom later would loosen the coachman's tongue soon enough. He threw open the parlor door with a flourish.

"There now, we've got a nice fire going. And when you are settled, Your Grace, perhaps a dish of tea? Mrs. Purdy has but a few minutes since taken a tray of scones from the oven if you would care to try one, with some of her special strawberry jam and cream . . . ?"

"An excellent idea, Purdy." He glanced at Serena. "Shall we say in about fifteen minutes?"

As the door closed behind the landlord, Serena looked around the small paneled room where the fire burned bright against the gathering evening and several lamps cast a softening light. She stripped off her gloves and held her hands out to the flames.

"How cozy this is," she exclaimed, feeling the need to talk in order to cover the sudden inexplicable awkwardness of being alone with the duke in a strange inn miles from home. "When I stayed here with Mama, the days were longer and there was no need for a fire . . ."

Cedric came and took hold of her hands, turning her to face him. "I daresay you are feeling a little strange, my dear." His smile was reassuring. "But it's only me, Serena, your harmless cousin, Cedric."

"Yes, of course." She returned his smile. "You must

think me very foolish. It seems to have been a very long day."

"If you would rather have tea in your room and rest for a while . . ."

For a moment she was tempted. But there was a hint of uncertainty in his voice, and she realized he was probably feeling every bit as strange as she. The knowledge moved her to exclaim lightly, "Heavens, no! I hope I am not so poor-spirited!"

And, almost imperceptibly, he relaxed.

Upstairs, in a room infinitely more spacious and comfortable than the one allotted to Mama and herself on her previous visit, she found a red-faced Bessie struggling to open the smaller of the two boxes that contained all that her mistress would need for the evening ahead, with a grim determination that was quite unlike her usual cheerful demeanor.

"Is everything all right, Bessie?"

The young girl looked up, and Serena saw at once that she labored with some strong inner grievance, and the sympathy in her mistress's voice brought it all pouring out.

"It's that Mr. Grove, Miss Serena. 'E's properly got the 'ump—got a face on him as would curdle milk! An' all on account of you being given the room as is usually reserved for 'Is Grace."

Serena ran a hand lovingly across the rich brocade quilt thrown over the bed, feeling the softness of feathers beneath her fingers, and noted the quality of the furnishings. No wonder it was so fine.

"Is that all? Well, we can soon put that right. I daresay there has been some mistake. Show me where he is, and I will go at once to tell him so."

Bessie shook her head vigorously, her dark curls bouncing. "Beggin' your pardon, Miss Serena, but that won't answer. Seemingly it's the duke hisself as has insisted that you should have this room on account of it's quieter, bein' at the back of the buildin'. An' Grove won't go against his master, no matter what."

"Oh, really! Then I shall have a quiet word with the duke."

But this didn't meet with Bessie's approval, either. "It's not for me to say, of course, but if 'Is Grace gives that valet what for, won't it just make matters worse?"

Serena was still pondering the problem as she entered the private parlor to find the immensely plump Mrs. Purdy vigorously shaking out a tablecloth that descended in snowy pillows to cover a table in the center of the room. She then proceeded to lay out an assortment of dishes that would fend off hunger for at least a week in anyone not possessed of a gargantuan appetite.

"Goodness, Mrs. Purdy! What a spread," exclaimed the duke. "You don't mean us to starve."

"I hope it's to your liking, I'm sure, Your Grace. I can't abide to see folk pick at their food, an' it's all good wholesome fare. An' it'll put you on. I've got trout fresh from the river, an' a nice brace of wood pigeon for your dinner." The empty tray clutched to her bosom, she bobbed an awkward curtsy, and as she turned to leave, saw Serena. "Come you to the fire, Miss Fairburn. You look as if you could do with a good warm. Just pull the bell if you needs anything more."

Not daring to look at each other in her presence, they waited until all sound had faded before collapsing into peals of mirth.

"I don't know about putting us on until dinner," Cedric gasped, wiping his eyes. "It'll more likely put us in bed with the stomachache."

"She will be mortally offended if we don't consume the

lot." Serena surveyed the dishes of scones and malted bread and seedy cake, and the cream and the jam, and groaned. "And supper still to come! Oh, Ceddie, whatever shall we do?"

"Eat what we can and fill every available pocket and kerchief and your reticule with the rest—feed it to the birds when we are well away from here," he suggested. "Dear Serena, it's good to see you at ease again."

The laughter had cleared the air of any lingering awkwardness, and she found herself telling him about the minor feud that he had inadvertently started above stairs. "Really, there was no need to give up your room to me."

"I wanted you to have it." There was a hint of asperity in his voice that she was beginning to recognize as evidence that he was not entirely without a will of his own, as his mother would like to suppose. "As for Grove . . ."

Serena looked up from pouring the tea. "Cedric, don't scold him, I beg of you. Caring for you is his life's work."

"True. But that doesn't give him leave to question my orders."

"He didn't," she said lightly. "Not in so many words. And if you mean to make a fuss, I shall begin to wish I hadn't told you."

He grinned suddenly. "You occasionally have a disconcerting way of making me feel about as big as Edward. I do hope you don't mean to be a scold."

She chuckled, and harmony reigned once more.

Chapter Seven

Serena was more tired than she had expected. In many ways it seemed more like weeks than hours since she had parted from her family, with all the distress that had accompanied the leavetaking. But the images still clouded her mind.

The room was certainly quiet. Serena hoped that Cedric would not be disturbed by the noise from the taproom. She moved the curtain aside. The window was on the first latch, letting in the cool night air, and she drew a deep breath that had in it the last lingering scents of the harvest. A sliver of moon pierced the blackness of the sky, and here and there a star winked. Would the same stars be winking over Mountford Grange? Somewhere an owl hooted mournfully. With a sigh she replaced the curtain and climbed into the blissful softness of the feather mattress where she floated in a kind of limbo, waiting for oblivion. Bessie had been gently snoring for some time when at last her own eyelids began to droop.

Something woke her, a sudden draught of air. The curtain was being quietly drawn back. In almost the same moment she heard a sound, the sharpness of indrawn breath. Her heart began to pound as she realized that Bessie was still snoring.

But before she could move, or even collect her thoughts,

she became aware of a shadow looming over her, and in the faint light from the window she saw an arm raised, the dull glint of something, a knife blade descending.

More by instinct than conscious thought, Serena flung herself to one side. There was a soft curse as the knife buried itself in the pillow. Feathers floated silently round her as the figure turned back, stumbling, cursing, scrambling over the windowsill.

And in that same moment Bessie woke up and began to scream.

"Do be quiet," Serena urged her shakily as she fumbled for her robe and dragged it on. "The intruder, whoever he was, has gone. Save your energies to try if you can light the candle."

As she spoke, there was a knocking on her door. She opened it and found the landing already alive with people, all tumbling from their rooms in various states of disarray and all talking at once.

Cedric was the first to her side, a lighted lamp in his hand, his green frogged dressing gown firmly tied, his fair hair slightly ruffled. "Are you all right? What has happened?"

She explained briefly and showed him the tear in the pillow and the window hanging open. He walked quickly across and peered out.

"No sign of life that I can see," he said, leaning out as far as he could.

"Your Grace! I beg of you, do come away from there before you take one of your chills!"

Grove, his nightcap askew, his feet bare beneath his nightshirt, and an expression of genuine distress creasing his plump features, seemed suddenly old and rather vulnerable.

"Oh, Your Grace, whatever shall I tell Her Grace if you ..."

Here words failed him, and Serena, feeling sorry for him, went across to lay a hand on his shoulder, her own panic by now more or less gone.

"Do sit here for a moment to collect yourself," she said, leading him to a chair. "Grove is quite right, Ceddie. Do shut that window, or we shall all take a chill. Whoever it was will be long gone by now. In fact, I am almost certain I heard the sound of a horse being ridden away at a gallop."

The landlord had by now arrived on the landing, and the other guests could be heard giving him various accounts of what had taken place, before being ushered back to their rooms to mutters of "disgraceful!" and "a man ain't safe anywhere these days!"

"There's a devil of a row going on out here, Purdy. What's to do, man?"

There was no mistaking that incisive voice. Serena stared at Cedric, who exclaimed, "Well, I'll be ..." and hurried to the door.

"Darcy! By all that's wonderful! Where did you spring from?"

"Ceddie! What the deuce is the meaning of all this racket?"

Lord Lynton stood in a doorway across the landing, looking almost incongruously elegant in a dark cutaway coat with turnback cuffs, immaculate cravat, and a pair of the newfangled black trousers, amid the noisy melee of guests in various stages of undress.

Quizzing glass raised, his glance strayed beyond Cedric, the heavy-lidded eyes narrowing as he saw Serena standing in the doorway of his cousin's room, looking so pure and innocent, her prim nightgown ill-concealed by the robe she clutched around her, her hair hanging over one shoulder in a long plaited rope. For a brief instant, his fingers itched to touch it, to loose it and watch it ripple over her shoulders.

"Ah!" The soft exclamation held a wealth of meaning. "You sly young pup, Ceddie. What *would* your mama say if she could see you now?"

Serena felt the hot blood come into her cheeks, very much aware of how open to misinterpretation must be her presence in the doorway of the room normally used by the duke—and in her nightclothes. But before she could speak, Cedric had turned angrily on Lynton.

"You'll apologize to Serena at once, Darcy, or answer to me—cousin or no!"

She found her voice then and with an effort kept it light. Only her eyes, locked into Lord Lynton's, betrayed her true feelings. "No quarrels, please, Ceddie. My conscience is clear, as yours is. As for his lordship, he may think what he pleases. It matters not a jot to me if he chooses to judge others by himself."

A momentary leap of anger in those hard eyes gave her all the satisfaction she needed.

"That won't suffice," the duke insisted stubbornly. "You have already suffered enough without having to endure insults from Darcy. When one considers all that has happened . . . how near you came to being killed . . ."

"Killed? What nonsense is this?"

"No nonsense, Coz." Cedric gave his cousin a forceful, if rather highly colored version of recent events and urged him to view the evidence, which he did briefly and without comment. "If I had not given up my room to Serena, she would not have been in such danger."

Lord Lynton was silent for a moment, then said slowly, "But you might well be dead."

They looked from one to the other in silence, broken by the landlord who had by now arrived on the scene, red-faced and apologetic, and hastily bundled into a dressing gown.

"I scarcely know what to say, Your Grace. This is not what I'm used to, an' that's a fact," he declared. "Though we get a rum crowd in the taproom on occasion—an', o'course, if any nefarious creature was to spy your rig in the stables, an' ask around, there's no knowin' what such a person would attempt once the drink was in him, this bein' your reg'lar room an' all . . ."

"Yes, well, no real harm has been done, Purdy, so I think any inquests can wait until morning. We shall all take a chill if we stand around like this much longer. Oh, and perhaps you could remove that pillow?"

"Indeed, yes, Your Grace." The landlord, recalled to his duties, gathered up the edges of the torn pillow and bowed profusely amid a little shower of feathers. "I'll see if I can rouse Mrs. Purdy to make a hot posset for yourself and Miss Fairburn. Sleeps like the dead, once she's off, does Mrs. P . . ."

"An excellent idea, Mr. Purdy, if it is not too much trouble," Serena said swiftly, seeing that Cedric was about to refuse. "In fact, I think hot possets all round would be most acceptable. And Bessie shall come down and help to carry them up."

"Yes, Miss Serena, o'course I will." Bessie, her spirits restored, had been sitting on her pallet, wrapped in a shawl, shivering. If there were possets to be made, she was going to make sure there was one for herself.

"Not for me," said Lord Lynton. He made Serena a brief bow before turning away. "I trust you will sleep undisturbed for what remains of the night, Miss Fairburn."

She looked for sarcasm, but for once found none. "Thank you, my lord. Ceddie, I think you should go back to bed, too." She lowered her voice. "Poor Grove looks quite done in."

"So he does. Come on, Grove, old fellow. Time for bed."

The eyes snapped open and the shoulders straightened. "Indeed, yes, Your Grace. I will see if I can procure a warming pan. The bedclothes will be quite chilled by now, I shouldn't wonder."

"Nonsense, I shan't take any harm." The duke smiled at Serena. "All's well that ends well, what?"

"Yes."

Serena watched him hurry after Lord Lynton. "How do you come to be here, anyway?" she heard him demand, his equilibrium restored once more. "You weren't here earlier."

"Quite simply, I was on my way home from a card party no more than a mile or two from here when one of my horses cast a shoe. It was late, but I reckoned old Purdy would still be around . . ."

Serena shut her door.

Rather to her surprise, she was awake at her usual hour, to the disappointment of Bessie, who had hoped to snatch an extra hour in bed. The young maid stifled a yawn as Serena sat up and reached for her robe.

"Lord, Miss Serena, you'll never be thinking of getting up so soon? I'm sure no one'll be expecting to see you for ages yet, what with all the excitement."

"Then I shall go for a nice brisk walk." She glanced out of the window. "There is a slight mist, but the sun will be up shortly, and I shall feel a great deal better for the exercise."

Bessie sighed and scrambled into her clothes. "You'll be wanting some water then. I'll go down to the kitchen and fetch some."

In a short time Serena was dressed and wrapped in her warm cloak, its hood edged with fur. There was no one in sight as she descended the stairs except Mrs. Purdy, who exclaimed upon seeing her.

"You'll never be thinkin' of going out, Miss Fairburn! That Bessie said you was awake, but I didn't expect to see you down so soon. That was a nasty experience you had . . ."

"Yes, but I'm fine now. And I shall be even better after some good fresh air. It will give me an appetite for breakfast."

Mrs. Purdy thought she was used to the ways of the gentry, but this young lady wasn't at all like most she'd had dealings with. "Well, I suppose you knows best, Miss. I'll have breakfast laid in the private parlour directly. His Grace usually rises much later and has breakfast in his room . . ."

"Then I'm sure that is what he will do this morning."

Serena set out briskly. There had been a light frost and as the sun came up, big and golden, it gave an added beauty to the landscape. She met no one but a farmer and his dog herding sheep from one field to another. She greeted him cheerfully, and he muttered a surly 'morning', obviously thinking her mad.

By daylight, the events of the previous night seemed less dramatic than they had at the time. The innkeeper was probably right—some drunken young villain, learning about the inn's prestigious guest, had decided to use the knowledge to his advantage.

As Serena arrived back, she caught a glimpse of Lynton's young tiger in the courtyard. He saw her and bobbed his head. She entered the parlor, her appetite sharpened by the cold air, to find a lovely fire burning and a delicious smell of coffee wafting on the air. Also, she had company.

"My lord," she exclaimed as the tall, elegant figure turned away from the window whence he had watched her approach. "I had not expected . . ."

He observed the healthy glow in her cheeks, which deepened a little on seeing him. Her violet-gray eyes were bright and clear, betraying no evidence of the traumas of the previous night as she put back her hood.

"You are not the only one who favors early rising, Miss Fairburn. Though I confess I am surprised to see you abroad so early on this particular morning." He paused, eyeing her intently. "Were you not apprehensive of venturing forth alone so soon after your ordeal?"

"Certainly not. I endured an uncomfortable few moments last night, but reason convinces me that what happened was a random attempt by a thief who is probably miles away by now. A poor creature I should think myself, to go round starting at shadows."

"You are very cool, Miss Fairburn."

"No, my lord. Just practical."

He stared at her a moment longer, eyes narrowed, then uttered a short laugh. "It seems Ceddie has done rather better for himself than I had supposed. Though I'm surprised the dowager sanctioned a match with so spirited a young lady."

"To be honest, so am I. I believe my Fairburn blood rather than any outstanding qualities in me led her to overcome her misgivings." Serena sighed. "And, of course, she means to remain to rule the roost."

"I grieve for you," he said dryly, though this time his laugh held a touch of sympathy. "Perhaps, since we are destined to be part of the same family, Miss Fairburn, we should call a truce."

"It would please Cedric," she agreed and held out her hand.

He took it thoughtfully, holding it far longer than was necessary. "I thought we might breakfast together if you have no objection?"

"By all means, my lord."

She loosened the clasp of her cloak and cast it aside on a chair. Her morning gown of dark gray chintz was severe in its simplicity, but it showed her figure to distinct advantage. Her hair was dressed in its usual neat knot, and once again he found his fingers itching to set it free.

He was wearing the clothes he had worn the previous night, and his chin had an unshaven shadow. He said in self-mockery, "I am hardly fit to be seen, as well as being a trifle overdressed for breakfast. But then, I had not expected to spend the night away from home."

"My lord, as far as I am concerned, you may wear whatever you wish."

"A challenging thought," he said dryly, making her blush, and sat down opposite her.

In the event, breakfast passed off without incident. Lord Lynton was polite, even surprisingly agreeable at times, so that Serena found herself relaxing in his company. By the time they were sitting back with a last cup of coffee, she felt sufficiently at ease with him to venture a question that had been troubling her.

"My lord, you seem to be on close terms with Cedric. Would you mind if I asked you about his health? Is it truly as delicate as Her Grace gave me reason to suppose?"

He sat back, regarding her with an enigmatic expression. "Why do you ask?"

"Because I believe it is important for me to know. The duchess impressed upon me at our first meeting that Cedric has a weak heart and must on no account engage in anything of an energetic nature . . ." Serena watched his expression change to a kind of sardonic amusement and blushed as she divined his obvious conclusion. But she persevered. "It is simply that during the past few days we have been riding quite a lot. Also, Edward has been quite demanding of him. I did try to discourage Edward, but Cedric would have none of it."

"And?" Lord Lynton sat forward.

"He managed rather better than I had expected. Grove is very protective of him, of course . . ." She heard her companion mutter "that old fool" as she continued, "Though not entirely without cause, I think, for there were moments when he tired quite suddenly."

"As you would if you were never allowed to exert yourself," the earl said forcefully. "Ceddie has been overprotected from the cradle. I don't deny that his constitution is far from robust, but I suspect that he is far from being such a weakling as my aunt would have everyone suppose. Frustration can be every bit as exhausting as physical effort."

Serena was beginning to think that she had misjudged Lord Lynton. He certainly appeared to hold his young cousin in a kind of rough affection. "I am glad to hear you say so. I shall have to consider how best to act."

"With the greatest care," he advised dryly. "You cross the duchess at your peril."

She laughed, a low attractive gurgle of sound. And then, as quickly, sobered. "About last night, my lord? You seemed very sure at the time that it was a random attempt at theft."

There was a small silence.

"Do you have any reason to think otherwise?"

Something in his voice made Serena hesitate. "Nothing that makes sense. Everything happened so quickly, but . . ."

"Yes?"

"Well, I had the distinct impression that, had I not woken at precisely that moment, that knife would have found its mark." Her words hung in the air. "And if Cedric had been occupying his own room . . ."

"Ah!"

"You think I am being fanciful?"

The earl pushed back his chair and stood up. "I think we shall never know the answer, and that you should put the whole wretched business from your mind." Unexpectedly, he smiled. "And now, I must be on my way. But you will see me again very soon. I believe the dowager means to have a gathering of her relations, by way of formalizing your betrothal." He bowed. "Have a safe journey."

Serena continued to sit in a mood of deep thoughtfulness, long after the door had closed behind Lord Lynton. Then she too got up to leave. As she passed the table, a faint movement caught her eye.

It was a tiny downy feather drifting across the tablecloth, precisely where, a few moments since, his lordship's arm had rested.

Chapter Eight

It was late in the afternoon when they arrived at Masham Court. Cedric had been silent for much of the journey, and Serena, noticing the lines of weariness in his face, made no attempt to engage him in conversation.

She suspected that the events of the previous night had shaken him rather more than he cared to admit, but he was adamant that his mother should know nothing of what had happened. And she, not wishing to be interrogated by the duchess, readily agreed.

Nevertheless, her thoughts, lacking direction, turned irresistibly once more to Lord Lynton. Had she overreacted to the discovery of the feather, which could so easily have lodged in his cuff while he was examining the damage caused by her would-be assailant? After all, he could have no possible reason for wishing to harm Cedric. On the contrary, he had seemed quite genuinely concerned about him at breakfast. She really must learn not to let prejudice affect her judgment. But in spite of her resolve, the niggling doubt would not be entirely banished.

The duchess received them coolly on their return, her back rigid as she awaited them in the crimson salon with Miss Pennyweather fluttering round her in attendance.

"I suppose that I must be grateful that you have condescended to return at all, Cedric; Pennyweather, do stop whatever it is you are doing, and sit down."

Amelia Pennyweather jumped and scurried back to her chair in the alcove near the fire. "I'm sorry, Elvira. Yes, indeed, by all means . . ."

"It has long been my opinion," the voice swept as though her cousin had not spoken, "that, in the general way, young people have no consideration for the feelings of others, but I had supposed that you were different: that the precepts of good manners I instilled into you from your earliest years, would have led you to spare me the very natural apprehension your prolonged absence has wrought in me."

Serena was very much aware that, although the words were addressed to her son, the duchess's frigid stare placed the blame squarely where she considered that it lay, with her.

Cedric roused himself to smile as he bent to kiss the unyielding cheek. "Come down from the boughs, Mama. I am not a child. Nor, I believe, can you question my manners, for I was most careful to send word that I was staying at Mountford Grange for a few days, and you know well enough that Grove cossets me like a nanny, so you had no cause for concern."

"Nevertheless, you are looking tired," she countered.

Cedric's conciliating smile grew a little set. "No more so than the effect of hours spent in a traveling coach would produce in most people, I assure you. I have had a most pleasant stay in Wiltshire."

"Nevertheless, perhaps you should go to your room and rest."

"Nonsense, I am perfectly all right."

"Well, we must hope there are no repercussions." Her Grace's basilisk stare turned once more upon Serena. "I trust you left your mother well, Miss Fairburn?"

"Thank you, ma'am. She is growing stronger by the day, though her spirits were understandably cast down at our parting."

"She will soon recover," said the duchess with that peculiarly single-minded disregard for anyone's feelings but her own. "She is indeed fortunate in having other children to console her."

"Ah, but none quite like Serena," Cedric was swift to say. "She will be sorely missed." And before his mother could comment further, "By the bye, Mama, we were honored with a visitation from Darcy at Mountford Grange."

"Indeed?"

"He expressed his intention of visiting Masham very soon."

"Do you say so?" The duchess was cool. "One might almost suppose he had been reading my thoughts, for I have not been idle in your absence. I have this day sent out invitations to the family for the second weekend in October, so that they may make Miss Fairburn's acquaintance."

"By family, I assume you mean our immediate family?" Cedric turned to Serena. "Have I told you about my disreputable Uncle Eustace? He is a regular dandy, one of the Prince's set. Used to be one of Brummel's cronies, too, before the poor fellow fell from favor and quit the country. As a rule he only condescends to visit us when the duns are on his back."

"Cedric, I think we may be spared your levity," the duchess reproved him severely. "Your uncle may be a trifle eccentric, but he is your dear late father's brother for all that."

"What a jolly party we shall be," Cedric continued, unabashed. "Aunt Charlotte won't care for him being here. I never saw a brother and sister so at odds with each other. And Darcy won't thank you for inviting Aunt Charlotte, either, especially if that fellow, Morville, is to accompany her. Darcy doesn't care for his mama's latest conquest—reckons he's a bit of a loose fish."

The duchess rose from her chair, all outraged dignity.

"That will be quite enough, Cedric. I will thank you not to sully my ears with such language. I can only imagine that tiredness has made you careless. Miss Fairburn, you also must be tired after your journey. We will discuss this matter later when you are both rested."

"Mama, can we not have an end to all this formality? If Serena and I are to be married, surely you can begin to call my fiancée by her given name!"

It was so unlike Cedric to succumb to peevishness that both women were taken by surprise. But Serena, seeing that he was a little pale round the mouth, was quick to agree they would both be the better for a rest, thus earning herself an unexpected look of something approaching gratitude from Her Grace.

It came as no great surprise to either of them, however, when Westerby, primed by Grove, later came to inform the duchess and Miss Fairburn as they awaited him in the Yellow Salon, that His Grace begged their pardon, but he would not be down to dinner. His Grace had the headache and had taken a dose of laudanum.

"There!" declared his mother, as if vindicated. "I knew he was done up with all that gallivanting! I had hoped you would have more care of him."

Serena said impulsively, "Cedric enjoyed his visit with my family enormously, which is why he was so eager to prolong it. Furthermore, I believe it did him nothing but good. Which leads me to wonder, ma'am, if he is not smothered with too much care. Cedric is not a child."

The bosom, encrusted with amethyst beading, swelled with indignation. "And who are you, Miss Fairburn, to pro-

nounce on such matters after so brief an acquaintance? You
have not sat beside his bed a hundred times, watching him
toss in a fever, willing him to cling to life!"

In spite of the hyperbole, Serena was aware of a quite
genuine distress behind the words. There could be no doubt
that the duchess loved her son, too much, perhaps for his
own good. This fact led her bite back a very natural inclina-
tion to continue the argument. On one point, however, she
felt constrained to voice her misgivings gently, but with a
very real concern.

"Does Cedric often take laudanum, ma'am?"

The question was received with astonishment. "No more
than anyone in his condition might be expected to do.
Grove is scrupulous in its administration, and Dr. Proctor
assures me it does Cedric no harm."

"I see." Serena, faced with the daunting prospect of dining with her future mother-in-law, with only Miss Pennyweather for support, decided that discretion was the better
part of valor, and offered no further comment. Nevertheless, it continued to trouble her that Cedric should be so de-
pendent on a medicine that their own dear Dr. Frank had
actively discouraged Mama from having recourse to on a
regular basis, for fear that she would not, in the end, be able
to manage without it.

However, by the next morning, Cedric was her charming
companion once more, so perhaps she had allowed herself
to worry unnecessarily.

In the days that followed, the great house became a hive
of activity as rooms not normally in use had their doors
flung wide to an army of maids who swept and polished,
and aired the beds against the imminent arrival of their
guests, who had all, to Cedric's surprise accepted, and
would number five in all.

"But one is a mere secretary, and doesn't really count."

"Good gracious!" Serena exclaimed. "All this work for five people?"

Cedric grinned. "Five, twenty-five, it makes little difference. When Mama holds court, which ain't often these days, she likes to play Grande Dame, as you will no doubt have gathered. This time, thank God, she has confined herself to my late father's immediate family."

"Even so, I shall be terrified."

"Not you, dear Coz. I can't imagine you being frightened by anything or anyone."

They were in his private rooms set well away from the main apartments of Masham Court, at the end of a long corridor that housed the muniments room and the gun room.

This was the first time she had been inside these private rooms where Cedric spent much of his time painting and cataloguing his butterflies and other species of small wildlife, so that this visit was a revelation, making her realize that until now she had seen only a small part of his work: the occasional picture hanging in one of the salons, books filled with sketches and neatly written descriptions of each species.

But here, the work seemed to take on a life of its own as she was permitted to study the exquisitely detailed paintings and drawings that lined the walls or lay scattered across the many desks and tables—some finished, some little more than a brief sketch of a wing fully open or part of a body.

"Oh, Cedric! I hardly know what to say!"

"Very little, I hope," he had returned swiftly. "Only a few people have been beyond that door, and that's how I want things to remain."

"Has your mama not seen all this?" Serena queried.

"She has never really taken much interest. Oh, she acknowledges that my paintings are really rather fine. I be-

lieve she has one in her bedchamber." His smile had a wry
quality. "Cedric's little hobby, she calls it."

Serena was outraged by this lack of true appreciation.
"But is there not some natural history society who would be
interested?"

He shrugged. "Probably. But I don't want a lot of strange
people tramping round the place. What I do, I do for my
own pleasure, so not a word to anyone, eh?"

"If that's how you want it," she agreed as he led her toward the door. "Though it does seem an awful waste."

"Not to me. Now, you haven't seen round the stables yet.
Come along and say 'good morning' to Starlight. The poor
fellow hasn't had much exercise since we came back."

The stables, like every other part of Masham Court, were
vast, incorporating numerous vehicles—everything from
the grand traveling coach to gigs and phaetons, to a wag-
gonette for use on the estate. Many of the stalls were filled
with carriage horses of all kinds, but right at the far end
were several thoroughbred riding horses. Starlight, hearing
his master's voice, thrust his head out with a welcoming
whinny.

"There you are, old fellow," Cedric said, fondling his
ears as the gelding butted him playfully before dipping his
head toward the young duke's pocket. "Is this what you're
looking for?" He brought out an apple, which disappeared
in a trice.

"It's time we did something about finding you a mount,"
Cedric said. "None of these are really suitable. What do
you think, Hurly?" He turned to the head groom who hovered nearby. "Know of anyone hereabouts with a horse
suitable for a lady? Something well behaved, but with a bit
of go in it."

"Matter o'fact, Y'r Grace, I might just know of an animal as would suit Miss Fairburn a treat," said Hurly, who

had taken an instant liking to the duke's young lady. "Colonel Malpas, over near Micklemirsh, had a couple of four-year-olds he was lookin' to sell when I was over that way last week—a bay, and a nice-looking gray filly. I can ride over there this afternoon—bring 'em back, so you can give 'em a look if he still has 'em—or Y'r Grace might care to drive Miss Fairburn over there yourself, bein' as it's a bonny day."

"A splendid idea, Hurly. We'll go this very afternoon, eh, Serena?"

"Lovely."

The duchess did not think it a splendid idea, however. "I had hoped that Serena"—the name came out with an effort—"would go through the arrangements for next weekend with me. I daresay she has had little or no experience of entertaining and cannot therefore begin too soon to learn what is involved in planning even the most informal of occasions."

Her Grace's habit of talking about her as if she were not present was beginning to irk Serena. "You are more than kind, ma'am," she said politely, but firmly. "I do realize I have much to learn, but a few hours here or there can surely make little difference? The days are rapidly growing shorter. We shall not have many more as perfect as today, and the fresh air will do Cedric so much good, don't you think?"

"I doubt I've ever seen anyone roll Mama up quite so adroitly," Cedric chortled as he drove them along the country lanes in a beautifully appointed phaeton, a sprightly black gelding between the shafts. The hedgerows were thick with berries, while above them, the mellow sunshine set the trees ablaze with every shade from gold to brown to red.

Serena was impressed with the way Cedric handled the ribbons and said so.

"So I should hope," he said with a grin. "Darcy taught me, and he's a devil of a taskmaster. Mama didn't care above half for the idea of my indulging in anything of an energetic nature, but by the time she found out, I was well on the way to being an accomplished whip. Can't hold a candle to my cousin, of course."

Serena remembered the way Lord Lynton had controlled his lively pair as they swept out of the gates at Mountford Grange in a cloud of dust. It was, as she had grudgingly admitted at the time, a brilliant exhibition of skill.

"I doubt his lordship cares to be bested by anyone," she said, and the tone of her voice made Cedric cast her an amused look.

"There are few who would attempt it. He doesn't suffer fools gladly. But you mustn't be put off by his manner. He's been devilish good to me."

Cedric pulled back a little on the reins. "That's the Malpas place up ahead if I'm not mistaken."

Colonel Malpas greeted them warmly, and in a very short space of time Serena had succumbed to the coquettish advances of Smoke, a beautifully behaved gray with a full swishing tail and soft doelike eyes. Her only riding habit had grown shabby with use and had several times been let out at the seams. A present from Grandmother Bradshaw, it was of brown broadcloth, the jacket beautifully cut, with a black velvet collar and matching buttons. Her hat was black and low-crowned, and she had recently ornamented it with a soft brown scarf.

No one seemed to notice its shortcomings, however, least of all Smoke, as she cantered round the field in perfect harmony with the animal, whispering sweet nothings in his ear, before returning to Cedric and the colonel, glowing with pleasure.

"She is a darling horse," she said, parting from him with

reluctance, though the colonel promised that his head groom would bring him over later that evening. "And you are a good, kind man. I shall be well and truly spoiled if you mean to carry on at this rate."

He threw her a quick smile. "Well, you'll have to get used to it, m'dear, for I've only just begun. Don't think I'm not aware of how long you've carried that family of yours, with your mama being the way she is. It seems to me, you are well overdue for a little spoiling."

She felt momentarily guilty as she realized that she hadn't thought about them once in the last few hours. But it had been such a perfect day it would be foolish to spoil it now. The family wouldn't begrudge her a little happiness.

The sun was a huge mellow ball that gilded the whole countryside as they approached Masham and saw a little way ahead a lone figure in a pale blue riding dress, sitting on a fallen tree trunk, shoulders drooping in dejection.

As they drew near, Serena exclaimed, "Why, she is but a child! Whatever can she be doing out here on her own?"

"Taken a toss, by the look of it." Cedric brought the phaeton to a halt, secured the reins, and jumped down.

At their approach the girl raised her head, and hair like spun gold shimmered in the setting sun as it tumbled about her shoulders. Serena heard Cedric catch his breath. And small wonder, for though young, this was no child.

The face lifted up toward him was nothing short of angelic in its purity of line from wide brow to sweetly pointed chin. Huge sea green eyes, thickly fringed, glistened with unshed tears, and more tears trembled like dewdrops on the pale curve of her cheek.

In that instant, before a word had been said, Serena knew that Cedric had fallen hopelessly, helplessly in love.

Chapter Nine

Serena's dismay and the jolt to her pride swiftly gave way to practicalities. As she hurried across, Cedric was already bending over the girl, speaking gently to reassure her, exhorting her not to be afraid.

"I am Cornwell, and this is my fiancée, Miss Serena Fairburn. Pray, tell us how we may help you. Are you hurt in any way?"

"How kind," she murmured, a catch in her soft voice. "I am not hurt, but I feel so very foolish." Even white teeth closed on a full, tremulous lower lip. "I was riding alone— something Papa has expressly forbidden me to do—when a rabbit shot out of the hedgerow right into Midnight's path! He is by nature the gentlest of animals, but in his fright he reared and unseated me, then galloped off down the road. When he arrives home without me, Papa will be in such a taking . . ."

"Well, that is soon remedied," Serena said bracingly as the voice began to tremble once more. "You have but to tell His Grace where you live, and he will have you home in a trice."

"His Grace?" Her eyes opened very wide. "Are you a duke?"

She sounded so surprised that Cedric laughed, and a faint pink flush stained his cheeks. "I am aware that I don't look in the least like one. But that cannot be helped. May we have the pleasure of knowing who you are?"

"My name is Melissa Glenville. My father is Sir Lionel Glenville."

"The magistrate?" Cedric exclaimed. "I'm sure he used to be a friend of my father's. I did not know he had a daughter. Why have I never seen you before now?" It was almost an accusation.

Miss Glenville's gold-tipped lashes fluttered down to veil her expression, but a delicate blush stained her cheeks. "I have been away at school for several years. My mother died when I was quite small, and Papa could not bear the house without her, so he let it and moved to another part of the country. I had a governess until I was thirteen, when we moved back here," the breathless explanation continued. "And that was when Papa thought I should learn to mix with girls of my own age and sent me to a seminary for young ladies near Bath."

Serena thought it time to end the touching exchange and said briskly, "Well, I think we should return you to your father without further talk, before he resorts to sending out a search party."

She rescued Miss Glenville's hat, which had fallen behind the tree trunk, a handsome blue confection with a curling feather. And then rather wished she had been less accommodating, for as the young girl arranged it with almost careless ease upon her golden locks, the sweeping brim framed her face so delightfully that Cedric could not tear his glance away.

One could hardly blame him. No man could remain unmoved in the presence of such exquisite loveliness. Nor was it Miss Glenville's fault that Serena herself was left feeling suddenly shabby and clumsy. She had never envied Emily her fragile beauty, and until this moment had never wished to be the kind of young woman that gentlemen rushed to protect. So she was quite unprepared for the searing shaft of jealousy that suddenly pierced her through. Oh, Heavens, she sighed. What a coil!

They were obliged to travel the short distance to the Glenville residence in the closest proximity, with Miss Glenville crushed between Serena and the duke. But, after an initial moment of embarrassment, she prattled away happily, showing no obvious ill effects from her tumble as she regaled them with her future plans.

"I was too young to make my come-out last year, but by next spring I shall be almost eighteen and my Aunt Constance, who moves in all the best circles, has promised faithfully that she will present me then."

"And shall you like that?" Serena asked.

"Oh, yes. I know I shall!" the younger girl replied, sounding very like Emily. "The girls at school talked about little else, and it will be such fun to have lots of nice clothes and go to balls and Almack's. Actually being presented will be quite terrifying, of course, but . . . Oh, do pray slow down, Your Grace, for we are almost there."

She indicated a pair of stone gateposts set back and almost concealed by shrubbery. They swept through and round a bend in the long curving drive. Ahead of them a splendid Tudor building came into view, fronted by a wide courtyard where a great deal of frantic activity was to be observed, with several grooms on horseback wheeling about and a large white-haired gentleman, very red in the face, issuing orders from an open carriage as they prepared to set off.

"There is Papa!" Melissa exclaimed. "Oh dear, what a state he is in. I do hope he will not be too angry with me!"

But it soon became clear that her doting parent was so relieved to find his child restored to him unharmed, that empty threats were the most he could manage as he alternately hugged and scolded her.

"Wicked puss!" he exclaimed. "You almost gave your poor papa a seizure when Potter came running to tell me that you had gone riding alone and that Midnight had come home without you! It will be bread and water for you tonight, mark my words!"

"Oh, Papa!"

"Never mind 'Oh, Papa'. Now, make your thanks to His Grace and his young lady, and then you'd better go and tell Nurse, who is in such a state, and has had you dead and buried a dozen times by now, I shouldn't wonder."

"I do indeed thank you, my lord Duke," Melissa said, eyes demurely lowered. "And Miss Fairburn, too. I am sorry to have given you so much trouble. You have been most kind."

"It was no trouble, dear young lady. I am only happy that we came along when we did," Cedric assured her with a shy gallantry. "I hope we may meet again soon."

"So kind," she whispered, and curtsied, and hurried into the house.

"Well, now, Your Grace," boomed the magistrate jovially. "So you're Rupert Rufford's son. I was at Eton with y'r father, y'know. A long time ago that was, though we kept up the friendship on and off until m'wife passed away." He sighed and shook his head. "Still, it don't do to keep looking back. I'm a poor host. You must both come in and allow me to thank you properly."

"You are very kind, Sir Lionel. Any other time, we would be happy to accept, but my mother likes to dine at seven o'clock precisely . . ."

"Say no more, Your Grace. I well remember Elvira's passion for punctuality." Sir Lionel cleared his throat. "Just allow me to say that I can never adequately thank you for bringing my little girl safely home. I daresay you will think me an overindulgent parent, but Melissa is all I have, you see. She is but seventeen and so like her dear mother ..." He took out a large red handkerchief and blew his nose.

"I understand. But all's well that ends well, sir, and we were only too happy to have been in the right place at the right time, were we not, Serena?" Cedric glanced at her, hesitated and added, "Perhaps, if you have no objection, I will call tomorrow, to ascertain that Miss Glenville has suffered no ill effects."

"By all means, Your Grace," boomed the magistrate, his joviality restored. "We shall be honored to receive you."

They drove for some time in silence. Serena knew all too well where Cedric's thoughts were, and her own were in a state of confusion. She reminded herself yet again that any man would have to be a block of wood to remain unmoved by such a vision, and Cedric, with his love of beauty must succumb more readily than most. She also told herself that infatuation was almost always a transient emotion, but a swift glance at her fiancé's profile was not reassuring.

"Well, that was all very satisfactorily concluded," she said as brightly as she could manage, to break the silence. "How fortunate that we happened along when we did."

"Yes." Cedric's voice betrayed the depth of his anxiety. "I don't care to think what might have been the outcome, had some unscrupulous character been before us."

"No, indeed. Such a bewitching creature must inevitably subject any man to temptation," Serena agreed, willfully rubbing salt in her own wound.

He made no answer, but his silence was answer enough.

The duchess was not pleased that dinner had to be kept waiting while her son and his fiancée changed, though her manner mellowed slightly during the course of the meal upon hearing Sir Lionel's name mentioned.

"Good gracious, I haven't seen Glenville for years. Odd, really, when one remembers that he lives but a few miles away. When your father and I were first married, he came here quite often with Grace, his wife—not a brain in her head, but an acknowledged beauty and an impeccable pedigree. Could have looked as high as she liked, but it was love at sight with the two of 'em."

The duchess shook her head. "Poor Grace died tragically young, not long after y'r father, and Sir Lionel went away for a while. Came back about six years ago, and it was soon after his return that he was made a magistrate, but though he was y'r father's friend, our acquaintance was never renewed." The duchess looked up. "The child take after her mother, does she?"

"Almost certainly," Serena generously conceded.

"She is exquisite," said Cedric simultaneously.

She looked from one to the other. "H'm. Well, I shall invite them for dinner one evening during the family's visit. The Saturday, I think. Speaking of which, Serena, I would like to go over some menus with you and Cook tomorrow morning. And we must check some of the other arrangements. I hope you have nothing planned?"

"Nothing specific. My lovely new horse will be arriving sometime during the morning . . ." Was it only this afternoon she had first seen and chosen Smoke? It seemed like a year. "But I do not have to be there to meet him," she concluded reluctantly.

"I should hope not, indeed," the duchess declared with some force. "Duty before pleasure. I learned that lesson at my mother's knee and have never forgotten it. I hope you will make it your watchword, too. Now, about this secretary of Charlotte's—so pretentious of her, for what she can possibly want with a secretary, I'm sure I don't know. She says he is the only son of a Sir Rodney and Lady Bickerstaffe, who has fallen on hard times due to his father's losing his entire fortune through bad investment. Such carelessness in the father does not exactly inspire confidence in the son. But then, Charlotte never had a grain of sense. Apart from which, I daresay it feeds her ego to have a baronet's son for secretary."

Serena glanced at Cedric, who grinned and made a little gesture of resignation.

"However, his family circumstances are not our concern. He will, as we have already decided, occupy that small room at the end of the long corridor near the east wing. I hope she will not be expecting him to eat with us. I thought, perhaps, the servant's hall, or perhaps a tray in his room . . ."

It was a long day, but sleep came hard that night as a vague depression settled somewhere in Serena's breast and would not go away. And the cause did not lie with the duchess.

She had no doubt she was being foolish, letting her imagination run away with her. Abby used to say that troubles always became magnified in the dark of the night, and, like shadows, vanished with the dawn. But she could not rid herself of the notion that Miss Glenville might turn out to be a very substantial shadow.

She was just beginning to drift into sleep when, for the first time since her return to Masham, she heard it again—the sound of galloping horses.

She ran to the window and pulled back the curtain. As her eyes adjusted, she saw them—two figures on horseback, bent low, riding like the wind through the trees away from the house. And this time she was sure they were no figment of her imagination. Serena did not want to get anyone into trouble, but surely there could be no legitimate reason for being abroad at this late hour. She decided that in the morning she would tell Cedric what she had seen.

However, Cedric did not put in an appearance much before midday, by which time she was busy discussing menus. He seemed pale, yet restless, as he watched for a moment in pensive silence, and Serena wondered if he had been taking laudanum again, though she lacked the courage to ask.

"Thought I'd let you know. Malpas's groom has arrived with the gray. I can see you're busy, but we can try him out after luncheon if Mama can spare you."

The note of irony went unnoticed by the duchess, but Serena, needing to talk to him, felt as though she were being pulled two ways. Before she could speak, however, he was moving to the door.

"Meanwhile, I'm going to ride over to Glenville's place to assure myself that Miss Glenville has suffered no lasting harm after yesterday's distressing experience."

"Do that, my boy. If you will wait a moment, I will write a note, inviting them for Saturday evening."

Cedric did not return in time for luncheon, and Serena supposed that the Glenvilles had invited him to stay. And after luncheon, something happened which put both Miss Glenville and the strange happenings of the night right out of her mind.

Serena had gone to change into her riding dress and was on her way downstairs again when she heard the unmistakable sounds of someone arriving. Unsure whether to proceed or draw back, she paused and heard a voice upraised as it inquired jovially after Miss Fairburn.

Serena picked up her skirts and ran down the stairs in an unladylike fashion that shocked Westerby, and, arms outstretched and all decorum abandoned, flung herself upon the tall figure in a distinctive blue frock coat, sash, and white pantaloons standing with his back to the light.

"Connaught! I don't believe it! Oh, how wonderful to see you! When did you arrive home? Are you back for good? Have you seen Mama and the family?"

"Steady on, Serena! Let me catch m'breath." His hands grasped her shoulders, moving her away a little, the better to see her. "Damned if I've ever seen you so full of bloom—and small wonder if all I've been hearing is true. Going up in the world with a vengeance, I believe."

"Oh, never mind about me. I want to hear all about your exploits." She flicked his splendid coat. "A staff officer! When did this happen?"

For an instant his face grew serious. "A couple of months ago. Wellington lost several of his aides, killed or badly injured at Waterloo."

"And you never wrote to tell us! Wretched creature! I bet Mama was puffed up with pride."

Serena shrugged herself free of his hold and tucked her arm through his, the only gentleman of her acquaintance whose six-foot-two frame comprehensively outstripped her—no, not quite the only one, she reluctantly admitted, remembering Lord Lynton. She turned to the butler, who waited impassively.

"Westerby, this is my brother, Major Fairburn."

"Major Fairburn." The butler inclined his head, his manner warming a little as he viewed the obvious affection between the two. He had never seen His Grace's fiancée so animated. "If I may say so, Miss Fairburn, the likeness is quite marked."

"Do you think so?" She leaned back to eye Connaught critically, secretly impressed by the red-gold sideburns. "I suppose we are rather alike, except for our coloring."

"Will the major be staying, miss? I am sure Her Grace will be pleased to welcome one of our country's heroes." She turned to Connaught. "Yes, of course. I hadn't thought, but, yes. You will be staying, won't you, Con?" He grinned. "If it won't put anyone out. My groom is walking the horses at present."

"I am sure Her Grace will be only too delighted to welcome one of our country's heroes as her guest, sir," the butler said magnanimously.

"That's settled then. And you can walk round to the stables with me, now, Con, and tell me all your news. I have a beautiful new horse and want to show him off. Westerby, if you see His Grace, will you be so kind as to tell him where we have gone."

They walked together in the sunshine, with the groom following at a discreet distance with the horses. Serena quite forgot how cross she had been with Connaught as he told her of his adventures—the close calls he had had during the final stages of the battle, which had earned him promotion to Brigade Major. But although he made light of it, there was no disguising the awfulness and the carnage.

"Did you see Papa at all . . . before he was killed?"

"Strangely enough, I did. I was sent for news of how the guards were faring at La Haye Sainte, and who should be defending a bridge close by, but Pa. He had come upon this handful of nervy Belgians who had lost their commander. They were in a blue funk and on the point of abandoning their post. He knew it was vital that the bridge be held as long as possible, however hopeless the task, but you'd never have thought it to hear him enthusiastically rallying them."

"How like Papa." Serena felt a lump come into her throat and swallowed hard. "And you? You weren't hurt at all?"

He shrugged. "A few grazes. You know me, a charmed

life. But I wouldn't care to go through anything so terrible
again. The duke was very cut up about the loss of so many
good men."

"Once we heard you were safe, we had rather expected
you home. Mama was so distraught. With scarcely a word
from you, I think there were times when she was convinced
that you, too, were lost to her."

Connaught had the grace to look embarrassed. "Never
was much of a letter writer. And there was so much going
on. You'd have thought that defeating Boney would be
enough to satisfy even Beau Duoro, but not a bit of it.
Nothing would satisfy the Great Man but to pursue his
quarry all the way to Paris, if need be, and we were all
swept along with him."

Of course, she thought. But that was Connaught, so very
like Papa. The army would always come first, without a
care for home. And, like Papa, one would always forgive
him.

He was looking down at her now, a little shamefaced.
"I daresay you must have had a pretty hard time of it at
home . . . after Pa's death?"

"Well, I won't deny that there were many times when I
wished that you had been there to lend me support. Mama
will not have told you what a fix he left us in, for she still
does not truly understand the half of it . . ."

"Is that why you are marrying Cornwell?" Connaught,
ever blunt, demanded.

It sounded so crude, put like that, but it was very like
Connaught to go straight to the nub of things. She told him
of their precarious financial state and how the offer had
come about.

"I was angry with Papa at first, but when the offer came,
how could I do otherwise than accept? As it happens, I am
really quite fond of Cedric, though his mama"—Serena

looked about her to make sure that they were not over-heard—"The duchess is a positive gorgon."

Connaught put back his head and laughed. "Oh, well, praise be you ain't marrying the mother."

"Don't be so sure. She has every intention of continuing to rule the roost." But Serena's mouth curved in an answering smile. "Still, I daresay I shall manage to hold my own."

He turned to look back at the great bulk that was Masham. "Ugly barracks of a place, ain't it? Still, big as it is, you shouldn't have too much trouble getting away from your ma-in-law. At a rough guess, I'd say the place is big enough to house Wellington's complete strength in comparative comfort."

They came at last within sight of the stables and were just in time to see Cedric arriving back. He was walking, head down, looking rather pensive, but his manner changed abruptly as Serena introduced the two men. She was interested and relieved to see how well they took to each other. Connaught, of course, dwarfed his brother-in-law to be, but Cedric, as when confronted by his cousin, seemed unconcerned by his lack of inches.

"Was Miss Glenville quite recovered from her escapade?" Serena asked lightly.

"Yes. She seems none the worse for it, praise be," he replied, but ventured little else except to say that Sir Lionel had been pleased to accept Mama's invitation.

Once the matter of her brother's horses and groom had been attended to, Serena urged them both toward the end stall where she knew Smoke would be stabled. As if recognizing her voice, the gray put her head out and whinnied.

"There, you see," she cried, running on ahead of them. "She knows me already."

Serena took a small apple out of her pocket and held it out on her hand. With almost finicky precision, the gray took it from her and allowed her to fondle his ears while the two young men looked on indulgently.

"I've heard a lot about you from Serena," the duke told Connaught. "It's a pleasure to meet you at last. You will stay for a while, I hope."

"Thank you. For tonight, at least. Must spend as much time with Mama as possible." Connaught, big as he was, looked suddenly sheepish. "Fact is, I'm due back in Paris next week." And before his sister could take him to task, "Orders from the Great Man. Seems he needs me to socialize with the Frogs—create a spirit of goodwill and all that . . ."

"Well, really! I do think the duke might have spared you for longer," Serena exclaimed, "after being so long away." And then, seeing his expression, she wagged an accusing finger. "There'll be a lady in it somewhere. There usually is."

He did not trouble to deny it. In fact, just for an instant he looked very like the cat that had the cream.

"I knew it! Who is she, Con? Someone beautiful, I'll be bound. You always had an eye for a pretty woman."

"Well, as it happens, Marianne is very beautiful. She is also the daughter of one of the new French aristocracy." Connaught glanced at the duke a shade embarrassed.

"Oh, don't mind Cedric. He's not at all vainglorious."

Cedric looked quizzical. "Am I not?"

"Well, you certainly don't have delusions of grandeur like your mama."

He laughed. "Oh, Mama doesn't have delusions. She really is a Grande Dame."

"Then I'd better mind my manners this evening," Connaught said drolly. "Wouldn't do to let my little sister down."

"Not you," she retorted, unimpressed. "I never knew a

lady yet, young or old, who could remain impervious, once you set yourself to charm her."

Cedric laughed. "I cannot wait to see how you deal with Mama. I would hazard that she will be your greatest challenge to date."

But Cedric had reckoned without his mother's pride in her Fairburn heritage, of whom Connaught was living and breathing proof. His looks were exactly as they should be, and the knowledge that Wellington had singled him out for special honors surprised the duchess not at all.

She stayed up much later than usual, becoming almost genial under the influence of Connaught's easy charm.

"You are in every way a credit to our family name, Major Fairburn, as was your father before you," she informed him graciously when he finished entertaining her with a heavily edited account of his career to date, being careful to drop a few prestigious names into the conversation. "I foresee a great future for you."

Cedric and Serena listened, entranced.

"It was a *tour de forces*," Cedric confessed as they saw him off the following morning. "I have never seen Mama so amiable. You may come again whenever you like."

Connaught grinned. "Thanks. I'll hold you to that. Actually, I do hope to get home again before too long."

"In time to give your sister away, I hope," Cedric said.

"And when will that be?"

Cedric glanced at Serena. "We haven't actually set a date yet. But my mother is thinking of sometime close to Christmas."

"Spring would be nicer." She didn't know what made her say it. They both stared at her as she blushed, adding hastily, "Though I suppose the time of year hardly matters since it is to be a private family affair."

Cedric said nothing until they had waved Connaught out

of sight. As Serena turned to go back indoors, he reached
out a hand to stay her.

"A moment, my dear."

There was an oddly diffident note in his voice, and she
looked at him in surprise.

"You aren't having second thoughts, are you?"

"Of course not," she said. "Whatever made you think
that?"

He shrugged. "I don't know. I just had a feeling—what
you said about spring."

"Oh, that! Think nothing of it," she said lightly. "It was
just a silly general comment."

"Ah. Yes, I see."

For a moment Serena thought she detected a note of disappointment. It wasn't like her to be fanciful, yet, she
couldn't entirely put it out of her mind. Any more than she
could dismiss that he hadn't once mentioned Melissa
Glenville since his return from visiting her.

Chapter Ten

The duchess's scathing comments concerning her late husband's sister had aroused Serena's curiosity, though she was prepared to discount most of them. The picture they presented seemed so at odds with anyone connected with Darcy.

Cedric had chuckled. "Wait and see. For once, as it happens, Mama does not exaggerate." But he would say no more.

Serena had taken particular care with her appearance, and Bessie had brushed her side curls until they shone and pronounced her violet sarcenet to be very becoming. She was as ready as she would ever be to meet Cedric's relations.

Even before she reached the half landing, she felt the draught as the great front door was thrown wide. And within moments she heard the sound of a great many people talking at once in the vestibule, and of Westerby's measured tones endeavoring to preserve an air of calm.

Her first sight of the Dowager Countess of Lynton was of a petite lady swathed in furs, her face entirely hidden by a dipping hat brim as she swept across the hall, giving a great many orders to the retinue that followed in her wake.

Immediately behind her came a soberly dressed young man of average height and indeterminate features, who carried a small leather case. The secretary, Serena decided, dismissing him as her interest was caught by the large, rather florid man who followed him—presumably the one who had been described by Lord Lynton as "a loose fish."

Serena hadn't been precisely sure what the term implied, but seeing him now in his "too, too solid flesh," she wondered what the dowager countess could possibly admire in such a creature, other than the fact that he was exceedingly wealthy.

Mr. Morville's coat, though it bore the stamp of a master tailor, was in danger of losing its struggle to accommodate a figure that outstripped it by several inches. His shirt points cradled a florid face and were so high he could scarcely move his head. And his tall beaver hat was set upon curling hair liberally anointed with Russian oil. To complete the incongruous picture, he carried beneath one arm a small and exceedingly bad-tempered pug dog who yapped and growled continuously.

"Hubert!" Lady Lynton's voice betrayed exasperation. "You are squeezing my poor Zoe. Don't hold her so tightly! Ah, Westerby, there you are. Such a journey as we have had! I am frozen and completely exhausted!"

"Indeed, your ladyship? I am very sorry to hear that. I hope we may soon have you feeling more the thing. There is a fire in the blue drawing room, where Her Grace awaits you, and tea will be served immediately." Westerby turned and saw Serena, and for a moment she thought she heard a sigh of relief. "Ah, here is Miss Fairburn, who will take you up."

The furs stirred, and wide luminous green eyes proceeded to look her up and down. "Lud!" her ladyship exclaimed. "Are you Cedric's bride? How tall you are! Quite Junoesque, in fact!"

Serena sensed rather than saw Westerby's mortification

on her behalf and stepped forward, saying pleasantly, "I am very pleased to meet you, Lady Lynton. Do let me take you up to the blue drawing room at once. I am sure you will be more comfortable there."

"You think so? I hope you may be right. I never was in all the years I lived here. One can only pray that there is an adequate fire. Hubert, come along, do. Westerby will see to everything. And Adam can supervise."

And without waiting for Serena to lead the way, her ladyship mounted the stairs, her voice floating back. "Did you see Cedric's fiancée? Such a beanpole she will look beside him."

So that is Darcy's mother Serena thought, following slowly. No wonder he is so difficult to fathom.

"Charlotte." The duchess greeted her sister-in-law coolly, but with meticulous politeness, the two women just touching cheeks. "I hope I see you well." Her voice grew positively frigid as she greeted Mr. Morville.

Her ladyship threw off her furs and removed her hat to reveal piquant features, too sharp for beauty, and suspiciously guinea-bright hair cut fashionably short.

"Hubert, give Zoe to me at once."

The animal was transferred with relief on Mr. Morville's part, for he could not but be aware of Her Grace's ill-concealed displeasure.

"Pray, sit down, Mr. Morville. Charlotte, you look chilled to the bone."

"I certainly am, after that journey. And must resign myself to remaining so, it seems," her ladyship said, lowering herself elegantly to the edge of a little brocaded settee, tucking the pug in beside her as she gazed pensively at the sight of the huge logs blazing in the vast fireplace and occasionally puffing out smoke. "This room faces east, of course. It never did get warm, as I remember, however many logs one threw on the fire. When one is accustomed to the greater comforts of a London house, one quite forgets how depressingly barren and cold a great mausoleum of a place like Masham can be."

The duchess was incensed.

"Nonsense. I have never found Masham to be either cold or depressing. Perhaps if you dressed more sensibly, you would not have cause to complain." She surveyed Charlotte's pale clinging gown that showed a great deal more of her sister-in-law's figure than could be thought seemly, with something approaching disgust. "I have never understood why you don't succumb to a congestion of the lungs. It is quite ridiculous, a woman of your age wearing such flimsy gowns! Pennyweather, pray give Lady Lynton your paisley shawl."

Miss Pennyweather half rose from her chair by the tea table, but was waved back somewhat imperiously by her ladyship, who declared that the day she was reduced to such a plebeian garment, she would retire to her bed.

"Humgudgeon!" retorted the duchess.

The footman, coming in with the tea tray, brought a temporary halt to this entertaining exchange of pleasantries. Serena smothered her disappointment, having every expectation that battle would be joined again before too long.

Cedric made his appearance just as she began to assist Miss Pennyweather in dispensing tea and was immediately subjected to a sweetly barbed interrogation by his aunt as to the advisability of his marrying at all.

"I was never more surprised, Elvira, than when I received your letter. Surely it cannot be either wise or advisable in poor Cedric's case? The strain, the responsibility, the . . . "

Before the duchess could reply, Cedric interjected in his deceptively amiable way, "Your concern is touching, Aunt

Charlotte, but you really must not worry yourself over my health or my future plans, you know." He reached for Serena's hand, and only she was aware that his trembled slightly, she suspected with anger. "I count myself very fortunate that Miss Fairburn has consented to marry me and am very much looking forward to my approaching nuptials."

There followed a pregnant silence. Then from the doorway came the sound of polite applause. Serena looked up to see that Lord Lynton stood in the doorway, an enigmatic smile playing about his mouth.

"A very pretty speech, Ceddie," he said and walked forward, bending to brush his mother's cheek with the briefest of salutations. "Mama, I hope I see you well?"

"Lud, Darcy. How you do like to creep up on one."

The irritation in her voice changed to reluctant pleasure as she glanced up at her son, clinging to his arm for a moment, her painted eyes widening appreciatively, lashes fluttering as she took in the cut of his coat, his long legs shown off to such advantage by the unwrinkled perfection of buff pantaloons. Almost, Serena was fascinated to observe, as if she would flirt with her own son—a kind of Oedipus manifestation in reverse. She set down her ladyship's cup.

"Tea, my lord?" she asked, her scrupulous politeness at odds with the sudden quickening of her pulse at his nearness.

"Good God, no!" Darcy withdrew his arm and stood up, raising an expressive eyebrow as she quickly moved away.

Cedric laughed. "There is Madeira on the bureau, Darcy. Mr. Morville, I am persuaded that you would prefer Madeira?"

"Too kind, Y'r Grace," he said effusively. "Indeed, that would be most acceptable."

Darcy moved with Cedric to the bureau. "I hope you realize what a sacrifice I am making by consenting to spend a whole weekend in the company of my mama and her tame monkey!"

Cedric summoned the waiting footman to take Mr. Morville's drink to him. "At least, thus far, she has shown no disposition to marry him."

"Oh, Mama ain't that stupid," Darcy said with deep irony. "She'll take his money for as long as it suits her, but never his name."

Cedric chuckled. "I suppose Lady Charlotte Morville wouldn't command the degree of deference shown to the Dowager Countess of Lynton."

"Quite so. Mind you, she is very expensive—all the unsecured money my father left her went on deep bassett long ago—so it's possible Morville will tire of being used eventually. In the meantime I am spared the necessity of having to pay her dressmaker and her gaming debts, to say nothing of her latest affectation, a private secretary"—his lip curled derisively—"for which respite, I suppose I must be duly thankful."

The more Serena listened, the more she realized that mother and son were not at all alike. Even so, she thought Darcy's attitude very unfeeling and was surprised to hear Cedric taking it all so lightly. She looked across at the countess, who was holding forth in her bright, spiteful way on the subject of her brother, Eustace.

"Lud, if you had but seen him last week at Madame Lieven's reception. I declare, his affectations grow worse!" Her brittle laugh trilled forth. "Hubert heard a rumor that his pockets were badly to let, did you not, my love? Is it true, Darcy?"

As Mr. Morville moved uncomfortably, her son shrugged and tossed back his drink. "My dear Mama, my uncle's affairs are of no interest to me. As long as he don't look to me to bail him out, he may do as he pleases. But, so far as I know, he hasn't yet been blackballed from White's or Waitier's, or any of his other haunts."

"Well, Hubert wouldn't know that, would he?" she retorted peevishly, "since he does not seem to merit entry to most of your favorite gambling hells."

"Charlotte, my sweet, I beg of you . . ." protested Mr. Morville. "It is not . . . You must not distwess yourself. I am sure your son has done evewything in his power . . ."

Darcy tossed off his drink, murmuring savagely, "There are limits, even to filial loyalty."

"Personally, I have never understood the compulsion to gamble," said the duchess, silencing them all. "But I thank God that Cedric's father did not, so far as I am aware, ever succumb to the Rufford family's apparent determination to throw money recklessly to the winds. A poor legacy he would have left his son, an' he had done so."

In the hiatus that followed this extraordinary pronouncement, a footman approached the duchess and bent to speak to her.

"Cedric," she said, "I believe your uncle has this moment arrived. Pray, go to welcome him."

"Come," Cedric murmured, taking Serena's hand. "This you must see."

At a nod of approval from the duchess, Serena left her place and went with him.

"I'll come along, too." Darcy's voice was brusque. "I need some fresh air."

They arrived on the scene in time to see a large chaise draw up, its springs groaning under the weight of a number of boxes and portmanteaus. The door was thrown open, and the steps let down, and after a moment a slim figure emerged. He paused to look about him, then proceeded to descend with mincing care. In one hand he carried a hand-kerchief and a long lightweight cane.

Sir Eustace Rufford was an exquisite of the first order. From the tip of his fashionably high-crowned beaver hat set upon luxuriant locks, to his topcoat adorned with huge mother-of-pearl buttons, to Hessians polished until they shone like glass, he was every inch a gentleman of the *ton*.

He was quite tall, as Serena discovered when he came to bow over her hand, but any notion that he was a mere frib-ble of a man vanished as he lifted his ornate quizzing glass. His face might be raddled, due no doubt to years of overindulgence, but as her eyes met his, she found them as-sessing her with a cold penetrating acuteness.

"So you are the Fairburn girl," he said enigmatically. His unwavering gaze took in every detail before he passed on. "And here is Cedric, too. So, do tell me, dear boy, when is the great day to be?"

"It is not finally decided, Uncle Eustace, some time just before Christmas."

"How very romantic." He shuddered delicately. "Let us go inside, children, before this demned icy wind gives us all a fit of the ague. Never could imagine why y'r mama chose to raise you in this draught-ridden heap, Cedric, when y' have other, more civilized establishments doing nothing. Speaking for myself, I couldn't wait to get out of it. Haven't been back since m' brother's funeral—and a demned freezing day that was! Put me in bed for a week."

Several footmen staggered past them and up the steps, under the weight of his portmanteaus.

"Humbert!" He spoke without raising his voice or at-tempting the delicate operation of turning his head. "Have a care for my bandboxes. Don't let these idiots get their hands on 'em."

The answering "No, my lord, as if I would," was accepted without a flicker to denote that it had been heard.

Upon reaching the vestibule, Sir Eustace paused. "Ah, Westerly, you are still here, then?"

"Yes, indeed, my lord. I am happy to see your lordship in good health. I have had your old room prepared."

"Well, I hope you've got rid of that cursed draught from the chimney," he said, proceeding to the inner hall. "What, Darcy, you here, too? And y'r mother, I suppose. Pack closin' in, eh? Well, I'd better get it over with—where are they all?"

"In the blue drawing room," Cedric said. "I'll come up with you."

"Very well. Better go and get it over with, I suppose. Humbert, you may take my coat and my cane."

The valet carefully laid down the bandbox he was carrying and proceeded to relieve Sir Eustace of his coat, revealing a cravat that was a miracle of complexity beneath a puce coat, a yellow waistcoat, and pale pantaloons.

"Serena?"

Darcy answered for her. "You go ahead with Uncle Eustace, Ceddie. I will look after Serena."

He laid a hand lightly beneath her arm, investing the gesture with a curious intimacy. On the first landing he held her back until the others were out of sight, before turning her to face him.

"So, now you have seen the worst of us. A charming family, are we not?" There was a curious intensity in his voice. "Does the prospect of becoming one of us not put you off?"

There seemed to be much more behind the words than he was actually saying. Serena tried to make light of it.

"Certainly not. I am marrying Cedric, not his family."

"Ah, if only it were that simple." His fingers perceptibly tightened their hold. "You do not love him, I think."

"I am extremely fond of Cedric and have every intention of making him happy."

"Noble sentiments." Darcy drew in a long deep breath, and when he spoke again, his voice seemed to hold the hint of a threat. "However, I must most urgently beg you to reconsider—if not for your own sake, then for Cedric's."

A small chill ran through her. "Indeed I will not. I cannot imagine why you should even suggest such a thing."

"I have my reasons—very pressing reasons." His voice softened persuasively. "I will engage to make it worth your while—to ensure that your family did not suffer."

"How dare you!" If he had not been holding her so tightly, she would have struck him. As it was, a welter of emotions were surging through her, most of which she couldn't even begin to understand. But uppermost was an anger so great, so unreasoning, she could not think coherently.

"Release me at once! Oh, this is insupportable, I thought you were Ceddie's friend! He certainly believes it to be so. What would he think, I wonder, if I were to tell him you were scheming behind his back, attempting to bribe me." Her eyes were brilliant with unshed tears.

"But you won't tell him, will you? And if you were so unwise as to do so, he wouldn't believe you."

"You are despicable!"

For a moment the look in his eyes terrified her. Then it faded, and he released her—put her away from him.

"Perhaps you are right. Forget what I said. And if you are wise, you will not mention this conversation . . . to Cedric, or to anyone else."

There was a note almost of pleading in his voice. She

swallowed a lump in her throat and drew herself up very straight.

"Oh, you need not worry. In that respect you were right. I doubt I would be believed. In any case, my most fervent wish is to forget that it ever happened."

Chapter Eleven

Y ou were very quiet at dinner," said the duchess.
"I'm sorry. I think perhaps I was tired," Serena answered, sensing a reproach.

If only Her Grace knew how great an effort it had been
for her to get through dinner at all. She was wearing a new
gown of dark mulberry silk, which the duchess assured her
would not flout any rules of mourning. "We are a family
gathering, after all." She knew that the color suited her,
bringing out the auburn tints in her hair, and that against it,
her pearls glowed luminously in the candlelight. But in
view of all that had happened this failed to lift her mood.

The evening had not begun well. Lady Charlotte had
swept into the salon where they had foregathered prepara-
tory to dining, her draperies floating about her, and had at
once taken the duchess to task for relegating Mr. Bickerstaffe to a paltry room at the far end of one of the draughti-
est corridors.

"And as for his being obliged to take his meals with the
likes of Westerby and Grove!"

"If that does not suit him, he may take them in his room,
other than at breakfast time, as my curate, Mr. Prost,
prefers to do."

"Really, Elvira. Julian Bickerstaffe has rather more address than a mere curate. He may have fallen on hard times, but he *is* the son of a baronet!"

The duchess had not taken kindly to the reprimand.

"He may be anything he chooses whilst beneath your roof, Charlotte, but you are at Masham now, and I am not accustomed to entertaining secretaries at my dinner table."

In the silence that followed, Serena had looked up to see Mr. Bickerstaffe in the discreet elegance of dark coat and breeches, being admitted by the footman. The duchess had a carrying voice, and having more than once been on the end of one of Her Grace's gibes, Serena could not but feel for him. But, apart from a rather white line about his mouth, the secretary gave no indication he had overheard the disparaging comment.

"Forgive my intrusion," he said formally as Serena moved to meet him. "But I have a letter that Lady Charlotte particularly wished me to prepare for her signature at the earliest opportunity. I had hoped to intercept her before she came down to dine . . ."

It was an embarrassing moment. The countess glared at her sister-in-law before hurrying across the room; Lord Eustace put up his eyeglass; Cedric moved uncomfortably; and Darcy viewed the whole proceedings with an air of cynical amusement.

The duchess had presided over dinner as though nothing had happened, but there was a lingering atmosphere. To Serena, still unnerved by her earlier encounter with Darcy, every mouthful she took tasted like sawdust, and although she tried to entertain Mr. Morville, who sat next to her, he had little by way of conversation, so that every nerve in her body was stretched as she tried to avoid eye contact with Darcy who sat next to the duchess on the opposite side of the table.

The situation was little improved when they moved to

the yellow salon to await the gentlemen, who seemed to linger rather longer than usual over their port. The little countess, so vivacious in the company of the gentlemen, reverted to silence as she prowled the room, her diaphanous gown floating about her restless body until the duchess commanded her to be still for five minutes.

"Are you quite well, my dear?" Miss Pennyweather whispered to Serena under cover of this distraction, her kindly face creased with concern. "I know people think I never notice things, but I can tell that you have not been at all yourself this evening."

Serena forced a smile. "Dear ma'am, you are very good and very perceptive. But it is nothing. Just nerves."

Miss Pennyweather glowed at the compliment. "Yes. Well, I daresay a degree of nerves is only to be expected. Such an ordeal as this must be for you . . ."

At that moment the door opened to admit the gentlemen, and Serena was spared a reply. Lady Lynton, coming miraculously back to life, greeted their return with relief.

"Lud, I thought you would never come!" she chided them petulantly. "Everywhere is so quiet here and so deadly dull! I had quite forgotten how the time drags in the country."

"I'm afraid we aren't up to your London ways, Aunt Charlotte," Cedric said. "I daresay Serena would be pleased to offer you a little music."

"Whist," her ladyship cut in abruptly, dismissing such insipid pastimes out of hand. "Surely, Elvira, you cannot object to us playing a rubber or two of whist. We can play for penny points. Eustace, you'll not refuse?"

He lifted a languid hand. "Anything to relieve the ennui."

"Good. And Darcy?"

"Not I, Mama. I am not in the humor for it."

"Nonsense. It will give your thoughts a new direction."
Her restless glance roamed the room. "And Hubert, of
course."

"Anything you say, dear heart."

"I will play if you wish, Aunt Charlotte," Cedric said unexpectedly.

"You?" Her ladyship's eyes opened very wide. "My dear
boy, I had no expectation of your being familiar with card
games."

He blushed slightly. "I don't play very often. But Mama
and I and Miss Pennywheather sometimes indulge in a rubber of whist if we can persuade our curate, Mr. Prost, to
make up a fourth partner."

"Pennyweather, too." Lady Charlotte made a quick cal-
culation and clapped her hands. "But this is splendid. If
everyone were to participate, we could run two tables."

"I think not. Cedric is tired." His mother frowned repres-
sively. "I believe you should retire, my dear boy. It has
been an eventful day."

"I don't feel in the least tired, Mama," he insisted with a
curtness quite alien to his usual compliant nature. "And you
can have no objection to an innocent family game of whist.
Serena, I know you play, for we had many a rubber when I
stayed at Mountford."

Knowing that she would be damned as a spoilsport by
her would-be relations if she declined, Serena said reluctantly, "I fear I would not be up to her ladyship's standard."

"Oh, that doesn't matter." The countess, full of enthusiasm, was eager to begin. "Now, let us put the names into a
pot, ladies first and then the gentlemen."

As a result of this, the two foursomes consisted of Eustace partnering Serena against Charlotte and Cedric, and
Hubert was drawn with Miss Pennyweather, while Darcy
partnered his aunt. Serena, relieved that she would not be

obliged to behave toward Darcy as though nothing had happened, settled down to give as good an account of herself as she could manage.

It was clear from the start that, to Eustace and Charlotte, it was not just a family game. Serena was soon out of her depth, but Cedric, to everyone's surprise, gave an excellent account of himself and almost snatched victory from defeat.

"You have been hiding your light, dear boy," Eustace drawled.

"Yes, indeed!" her ladyship exclaimed. "Wicked boy, letting us think you a veritable beginner!"

"Mere luck, dear Aunt," he said, and Serena saw that he was at last beginning to tire. She put out a hand to cover his, and he smiled his gentle smile.

From the other table the duchess could be heard constantly overruling her partner and questioning the decisions, and complaining to Darcy when the run of the game went against her. Finally, with the game all but won, her voice rose in damning accusation. "Pennyweather, you have trumped my king!" and Miss Pennyweather's gentle, but triumphant rejoinder, "Yes, Elvira, so I have!"

It was perhaps fortunate that the tea tray arrived before an argument could ensue.

"If anyone would care to take a gun out in the morning, our keeper, Palfry, will be pleased to accommodate you. The partridge are particularly plentiful at present, I believe."

"I wouldn't mind a little sport, as long as we don't have to set out too demned early." Eustace lifted heavy eyelids to his nephew. "What say you, Cedric? About eleven o'clock?"

"Oh, count me out, Uncle," Cedric said abruptly. "I study wildlife. I don't kill it for pleasure."

A small silence ensued before Eustace said, "Dear me."

"How quaint," Charlotte murmured.

"Cedric's health would not in any case permit him to be out in all weathers," his mother was quick to assure them by way of mitigation.

"I wouldn't mind twying my hand," Mr. Morville offered. "How about you, Darcy, my boy?"

The earl, who had seemed vaguely amused by the direction of the conversation, was noncommittal. "I may well join you later."

"We have guests for dinner tomorrow evening, by the way—Sir Lionel Glenville and his daughter. Sir Lionel is a magistrate. We have not seen him since his wife died. Very tragic. But the daughter is charming, so I'm told."

Sir Eustace stifled a yawn.

Serena slept fitfully that night and was up while Bessie was still rubbing her eyes.

"Lord, Miss Serena, you en't arf one for being up of a morning." She sniffed the cold air and, shivering at the thought of all those freezing passages and stairs to be negotiated in the half dark, said reluctantly, "I suppose you'll be wanting some water."

"Not just now. I feel in need of some fresh air, so I shall take Smoke out for a canter across the fields. I'll wash and change when I get back."

But, early as she was, she was not the first to the stables. Lord Lynton's groom, Grayson, was already leading out a large chestnut hunter. The man looked surprised to see her, and Darcy, noting his surprise, turned.

"Well, good morning. You couldn't sleep, either, I take it," he said, observing the dark rings beneath her eyes and the pallor that, even as he watched, became interestingly tinged with pink.

"I frequently wake early," she replied curtly, very much aware of her shabby riding dress and not wishing him to witness her sad lack of expert horsemanship. "But you need not feel obliged to bear me company. Your horse is clearly longing to gallop, and I am but an average rider and will only hold you up."

"Nothing of the kind. Prince is far too well-mannered to complain," he replied and continued to walk his well-disciplined hunter round the yard until Smoke was saddled and brought out to the mounting block. The mare was frisky and wanting to be off, and it took some moments to bring her under control—moments when Serena was mortifyingly aware of being watched.

"I did warn you, so on your own head be it," she said stiffly when at last they were out of the stable yard and cantering through the pasture land beyond. "My previous experience has been largely confined to exercising young Harry's mount in his absence."

"Never make excuses, Miss Fairburn," he told her equably. "It is the surest way to draw attention to your shortcomings and will either invite specious flattery or oblige people to lie in their teeth, neither of which is to be desired."

When she made no reply, he glanced across at her. "And now I have offended you again. I can almost see you biting back your desire to come to cuffs with me."

Her unwilling laugh had an edge. "You do seem to have a knack of putting me out of countenance, my lord."

"That is fair comment. In fact, it errs on the generous side, bearing in mind our last unfortunate encounter, for which I can only beg your pardon yet again."

He fell silent and she, embarrassed, could find nothing to say.

They rode on at a gentle pace, and the only sound to disturb the early morning air was the thud of the horses hooves on the damp earth. The autumn sunrise was turning the countryside to bronze and gold, and the beauty of the landscape made Serena think of home and brought a lump to her throat.

"Miss Fairburn?"

Her answer was muffled. She felt him glance at her, then heard him swear softly.

"Don't," he begged her. "I am not worth crying over. If my recent behavior has given you such a disgust of me that you cannot bear to be in my company, then I will leave you."

She put up a hand. "No, please! It is nothing you have said or done, my lord." Her throat was constricted, but she persevered. "I am not usually so idiotish. But my situation has not been easy these last weeks, and now . . . well, at the risk of being thought fanciful, I sometimes find that nature has a way of putting everything into perspective."

"In what way, precisely?"

"You will notice how the sunlight gilds the top branches of that tree? We have a tree very like that one at home, and it set me remembering. Abbey, our governess, used to say that whenever our anger got the better of us, we should go out and study that tree, which had been there, steadfast and strong in spite of wind and weather, since long before we were born, and would be there long after we had gone."

"Your governess has an irresistible approach to philosophy, Miss Fairburn," he said.

"There, you see," she returned with spirit. "I knew you would make fun of me. But I don't care."

He hardly gave the tree a glance, for at that moment her face, uplifted to the sun, was touched by the same golden light. He had not until now thought her beautiful, but in that light, the clean lines of brow and cheek and jaw had their

own kind of beauty. Damn! he thought savagely. What am I
doing here when I had vowed not to get involved?

"Come. Time to try that gray of yours in a gallop."

They raced across the fields. Serena was half scared, half
exhilarated, but Smoke behaved beautifully, responding to
her touch. And Darcy, fitting his chestnut's pace to hers,
was always there to control the gallop, so that it didn't get
out of hand.

"That was wonderful! I wouldn't have believed anything
could be so invigorating!" she exclaimed, her complexion
glowing as they slowed again to a canter and turned for
home.

When he did not answer, Serena glanced across at him
and found him looking straight ahead, his profile proud and
unyielding. Disappointment, like a current of cold water,
flooded through her.

"My lord?"

He turned, as if suddenly becoming aware of her presence, his expression inscrutable. "About what happened
yesterday . . . I am aware that an apology is scarcely adequate. At the very least, I owe you some kind of explanation."

Perversely, she didn't want to be reminded. She hadn't
wanted the magic to end. But already the golden sun was
fading to a watery pallor, and the bare trees resumed a win-
try aspect.

"Can we not simply forget what happened yesterday, my
lord?"

A smile briefly lit his eyes. "Heaping coals of fire?"

"No. Not that," she insisted. "But, as part of a large family, I have learned that it is sometimes better not to rake
them over unnecessarily."

"Perhaps you are right."

In an attempt to change the subject, she said impul-

sively, "My lord, there is a matter on which I would like to
... to ask your opinion. You will probably think me very
foolish ..."

He smiled wryly. "You are many things, Miss Fairburn,
but seldom, I think, foolish."

She blushed. "Do you think you could stop calling me
'Miss Fairburn' in that rather formal way? I find it rather
unnerving, and as I am so soon to marry Cedric, it would
surely be quite proper for you to call me Serena?"

"If that is your wish. On one condition—that you stop
addressing me as 'my lord'. Darcy will do very nicely." He
turned toward her and saw the tide of color surge anew in
her face. "Is that what you wished to ask me?"

"No, not at all. That was just ... oh, never mind." She
was already wishing she had never begun. "My lord ... I'm
sorry. Darcy, do you know of any reason why anyone
should go riding here quite late at night and with some degree of urgency?"

He pulled up short, and she, taken by surprise, hurriedly
reined in her own horse.

"What precisely are we talking about?" he asked, his
eyes searching her face. "I can, of course, think of any
number of reasons why the stable lads might occasionally
slip away—the lure of a pretty servant girl down in the village—a cockfight ..."

"Yes, I thought of that, too, of course. Only ..." she told
him what she had seen. "They didn't seem like servants.
There was something about them, the horses, too—a thoroughbred quality, I suppose, about the way they moved."
When he didn't answer, she sighed. "It sounds like the
worst kind of gothic novel, does it not? I knew you would
think me fanciful."

"I haven't said so. Has it happened recently?"

"Not for a while, until last night."

"And have you ever heard or seen the riders return?"

Serena shrugged. "No. I have tried to stay awake, but . . ."

"I see. Well, leave it with me, and I'll give it some thought. It could, of course, be Cedric himself slipping out in search of late-night pleasures."

"Darcy, if you mean to be facetious, I shall regret telling you."

"I'm glad you did," he said slowly, almost as though he were thinking aloud. "It may be something and nothing, of course. But ever since my aunt took it into her head that Ceddie should marry, I have been uneasy. My behavior yesterday, to which you so rightly took exception, was a clumsy attempt to prevent a possible tragedy."

"Darcy, you are talking in riddles."

As they came in sight of the stables, he slowed his horse to a walk and Smoke followed suit.

"If only the duchess had not been so obsessed with perpetuating the direct line. In so doing, she may have unwittingly set in train a whole series of events that could end in disaster."

"Are you not being a trifle melodramatic?" she said stiffly. "Of course, I can hardly fail to be aware that you think I am not good enough for Cedric, but . . ."

He looked up, surprised, and his laugh was harsh. "My dear girl, if that were all, there would be no problem."

She was so surprised that any anger she might have felt was swallowed up in curiosity, and she pressed him for an answer without feeling in the least in awe of him. "Well, then?"

He hesitated and then, reluctantly, began to speak. "I suppose it was seeing us all together yesterday that made me suddenly uneasy. I mean, why should Mama or Uncle Eustace put themselves out to agree to this visit? They both heartily dislike Aunt Elvira, and I doubt if they have seen Cedric since he was in short coats."

"Does it matter why they came?" Serena asked, not understanding. "Families do tend to get together on special occasions."

"Not this family. Cedric's father's funeral was the only time I ever saw them here. And they only came then because they believed there would be something to their advantage in his will."

"I am sure you should not speak to me of your mama in such disparaging terms."

"My dear girl, you have seen what she is like—selfish to the core. Oh, she is all over me now when it suits her, but it was not always so." There was so much bitterness in his voice that it almost frightened Serena. "I was an only child, you see, and my father was a solitary man, who died before I ever really got to know him. Mama spent most of the year in London, and I was raised almost entirely by nannies and tutors, no more than a dozen miles from here at Lynton Hall . . ."

Serena felt a rush of pity for that little boy who must have been so lonely and starved for affection. It probably accounted for the way he now viewed the world.

As if reading her thoughts, he said dryly, "This is no sentimental story devised to engage your pity, Miss Fairburn, for although I was a solitary child, and most likely a selfish one, I don't recall being particularly unhappy. I merely wish to set the background."

Serena bit her lip. "Yes, of course. Though I still think it no way to bring up a child."

Darcy half smiled. "That's as may be. Anyhow, I was about thirteen when Uncle Rupert died, by which time I was aware that Uncle Eustace and Mama had sponged off him for years. I wasn't actually present at the reading of the will, but the whole house was privy to the row that erupted when they discovered Rupert had left them nothing—that everything excluding the monies necessary for the running of the estate, to be administered by the duchess and the agent, had been left in trust for Cedric."

Serena found this background to the family fascinating, but she still didn't see what it had to do with her marriage to Cedric.

His expression remained too inscrutable to read. "My dear Miss Fairburn, have you any idea what the Cornwell Estates in total are worth?"

"None whatever. And I wish you would stop addressing me in that ridiculous formal way." She ignored his half smile. "Naturally, I realize the amount must be sizable."

Darcy named a sum that made Serena catch her breath. She inadvertently dug her heels into Smoke's sides, and the gray whinnied and took off, and a minor chase ensued.

"Truly, I had no idea!" she confessed when order had been restored. She stared across at Masham Court with new eyes. "I mean, just looking at that ugly pile, you would never believe it."

"Quite. But Masham, though the official Cornwell home, is but a small part of the whole estate, which is reckoned to be the sixth wealthiest in the country." Darcy paused for effect before continuing. "However, the will had a codicil, and this is where I believe danger may lie. In the event of the line dying out with Cedric, the estate is to be divided equally between his mother, my mother, Uncle Eustace, and myself."

He allowed the full impact of this to sink in, before concluding softly, "Even a quarter share of such an estate would be a prize worth killing for, wouldn't you say?"

Chapter Twelve

With so much to be done, Serena had little time to brood on what Darcy had told her, though it lay at the back of her mind like an incipient migraine and inevitably colored her view of their guests.

The gentlemen had breakfasted early and departed for the shoot, though Sir Eustace was less than enthusiastic, and had been heard to murmur that Morville was known to be demned dangerous with a gun in his hand.

Lady Lynton did not put in an appearance until after midday, when she repaired to one of the small salons where a light luncheon had been laid out. The gentlemen's needs had already been more than adequately catered for, and they were not expected to return much before dark.

Her ladyship was none too pleased to find only Miss Pennyweather to bear her company. Having met the woman's earnest inquiry as to whether she had passed a comfortable night with a catalogue of complaints and an assertion that she had scarcely closed her eyes, she further expressed her displeasure by picking up a copy of the *Ladies' Monthly Museum* and perusing it as though she did not exist.

Serena, coming in at last with Cedric, found them thus, and in spite of her misgivings, had the greatest difficulty in resisting the desire to succumb to a fit of the giggles.

"I am sorry not to have been here sooner," Serena said. "There has been a minor crisis in the kitchen, and I was obliged to smooth Cook's feathers."

"I have never believed in pandering to the servants," said the Countess. "It gives them a vastly inflated idea of their own importance."

"I daresay. But Her Grace treasures Mrs. Burton's skills, and if we were not to be left without dinner tonight, something had to be done." Lady Charlotte looked disposed to argue, and Serena deduced that it would be wise to change the subject, but when she said that she would arrange for luncheon to be served, the suggestion met with a frosty stare.

Cedric, seeing Serena's dilemma, came to her aid. "Mama will be here directly, Aunt Charlotte, but she told me most particularly that we are not to wait for her." He smiled his most charming smile. "I know you are partial to a glass of ratafia, and perhaps you could manage a little cold ham—and one of Cook's special patties?"

Her Grace arrived at that moment and having summed up the situation with a glance, proceeded to coerce her sister-in-law into submission.

Sir Eustace returned ahead of the main party, and after exchanging the briefest of pleasantries, announced his intention of changing his clothes and taking a drive.

The Duchess raised a disapproving eyebrow.

"As you will, Eustace. Though I cannot imagine where you would be wishing to go at such an hour. I hope you will not forget that we dine at seven, and have guests for the evening."

He gave her a heavy-lidded stare. "My dear Elvira. Tiresome as it is to be obliged to be polite to strangers, I shall return to do my duty. I hope I know better than to spoil your little dinner party."

He vouchsafed no reason for his unexpected behavior, which put her in a ferment of curiosity as to where he could possibly be wishing to go at such an hour, with the day already closing in. And he, knowing her frustration, smiled his thin smile and left the room.

"Really, Charlotte!" she declared, the moment he had left the room. "Your brother's manners grow worse with the years."

"As does your memory, Elvira," Lady Charlotte returned spitefully, "for he never possessed any that I recall, even in his youth."

Darcy had also quit the shoot early and now watched from the shelter of the trees as the coachman brought Lord Eustace's chaise to a halt on the forecourt.

A moment later, the undergrowth rustled close by, and Darcy's man, Grayson, came alongside him leading Prince, with Jack riding just behind on a sturdy pony.

"You certain you won't be wanting me along, m'lord?" Grayson muttered, casting a mistrustful eye at Jack. "A slip of a lad like 'im won't be much use to you if you was ter get into a fix."

"I have no intention of getting into a fix as you so eloquently put it, Grayson. I merely wish to satisfy my curiosity with regard to certain matters. All I require is someone to keep their eyes and ears open, and if necessary, to ferret out information, and who better for such a task than an inconspicuous bit of a lad like Jack?"

"I en't incon . . . what you said, Guv," Jack said, aggrieved.

"Well, I suppose you know what you're about," Grayson murmured, unconvinced. "But who's goin' ter watch your back, that's what I want to know."

"What a very poor opinion you have of my ability,

Grayson. I have no anticipation of needing my back watched at this precise moment. If ever I do, I promise you will be expected to play your part." He saw that the chaise was moving off. "Meanwhile, you could keep a discreet eye on my young cousin. There is always the possibility that our quarry may be cleverer than we take him for."

"Very good, m'lord."

Darcy followed at a distance, moving among the trees that skirted much of the land adjacent to the drive that wound for more than a mile to the main gates. There the chaise turned toward the village and presently drew up outside the Dog and Partridge Inn to allow Lord Eustace to alight at the front entrance before driving on into the inn's yard.

There was a large gateway giving access to the cellars on the nearside of the inn, which was used by the brewers' drays, and along the wall there was an iron tethering rail.

"Right, Jack. We'll leave the horses here. Don't want anyone in the main courtyard taking an interest, do we? And you get along to the taproom."

"Right, Guv."

"Don't draw attention to yourself. No doubt his lordship's driver will want to slake his thirst. Just keep your head down and watch and listen."

"Yer don't 'ave ter tell me, Guv." The lad grinned. "Werry good at bein' invisible, me."

"And don't pick any pockets, my lad, or I'll flay you alive."

"Guv!"

The reproachful tones cut no ice with Darcy. "Just a friendly warning, Jack. Get along now."

He waited until the boy was out of sight before sauntering in through the front door. There was no sign of Eustace, but then he hadn't expected him to advertise his presence.

However, a coin pressed into the right palm and a brief description brought instant results.

The gentleman concerned had not a moment since stepped into the back parlor with a friend who was staying at the inn—a very personable young gentleman, as polite as you could wish. A further coin elicited the information that young Mr. Marsden's room had been booked for an indefinite period.

"If you was wanting a word, sir, I could take a message?"

"No. It is of no importance," Darcy said carelessly.

He was still debating whether he dare risk trying to catch a glimpse of Marsden when the parlor door opened. He stepped back into the shadows as the two came out, the younger man leading the way.

He was not quite as tall as Eustace, but his coat was undoubtedly one of Weston's, his small clothes were immaculate, and he had fair hair styled à la Brutus. As he led the way toward the upper floor, he turned back with a trill of laughter in response to some remark Eustace had made, and Darcy saw that his skin was as smooth and fair as a girl's.

So that was the way of it.

It was no secret in the London clubs they both frequented that Eustace's taste ran to pretty boys rather than women. But, since he did not anticipate staying at Masham above a night or two, why risk bringing this particular lover here, thus risking the duchess's wrath, should she find out? Unless he was so enamoured that he could not bear to have the boy out of his sight for even a few days. There was no accounting for taste.

When Jack finally appeared, he had little new to offer.

"Mind, a few of the locals was havin' a good laugh. Seems 'is lordship's pickin' up the tab for this pretty young f . . ."

"Thank you, Jack. I had discovered that much for myself."

"Well, you did arsk me ter keep me eyes an' ears peeled," the boy muttered, aggrieved.

"So I did, and you have done so admirably, and may continue to do so. But you will tell no one else what you see or hear. No one at all. Do you understand me?"

" 'Course I do, Guv. Quiet as the grave, me." When his lordship used that tone, you didn't cross him if you valued your hide.

Serena faced the hours ahead with more nerves than she could account for. It was certainly trying to be obliged to endure a further evening of Cedric's relations, especially after what Darcy had told her that morning. Yet, much as she disliked them, she could not bring herself to believe any of them capable of attempting to harm Cedric.

Her present agitation, however, arose from quite another cause. And much as she told herself that Melissa Glenville was little older than Emily, and, judging from their admittedly brief acquaintance, seemed every bit as naive, Serena could not rid her memory of the expression on Cedric's face when first he saw her.

I am being very foolish, she told herself. Looks are not everything, and it is not as though we were passionately in love. Cedric and I complement one another very well, and he needs someone strong to care for him and shoulder some of the responsibilities he will one day be obliged to face. And I have a duty to my family.

But all the reasoning in the world could not quite quell her agitation as she dressed for dinner that evening. It seemed more than usually important that she should look her best.

The lavender-gray silk gown she had made just before

leaving home had certainly turned out well. She had edged
its brief bodice and puffed sleeves with tiny lavender flowers, and with its slim skirt the overall effect was of simple,
uncluttered elegance. Her eyes seemed like large violet
pools in her pale face, and her hair had been washed and
brushed until it shone. Around the high knot she wore another circlet of lavender flowers, from each side of which
tumbled clusters of ringlets.

"I've never seen you look bonnier," Bessie enthused.
"You've got lovely eyes, Miss Serena, an' if you'd just let
me dust a little rouge on your cheeks, they'd sparkle even
more."

Serena smiled, encouraged by the maid's enthusiasm as
she slipped the rope of pearls carefully over her head.

"Thank you, Bessie. But I shall have color enough by the
time I have fulfilled all my duties."

The whole family were assembled in the Yellow Salon to
await the arrival of Sir Lionel and his daughter. Sir Eustace,
in a coat of cherry velvet, intricate muslin cravat, and black
small clothes, restlessly prowled the room in shoes with the
largest gold buckles Serena had ever seen. Mr. Morville
was almost as flamboyant, but less impressive, and Darcy,
as always was the epitome of understated elegance in severe black and white. Cedric almost matched him, but was
clearly nervous and tugged occasionally at his cravat.

He smiled in some relief as Serena entered the room and
moved to her side. "You are looking very beautiful," he
said with absolute sincerity. And at once she felt better.
Even a sardonically quirked eyebrow from Darcy, who had
overheard the remark, failed to dim her pleasure.

Of the ladies, the duchess was in her favorite purple,
richly embroidered, and wore a feathered toque. And Lady
Charlotte had excelled herself in a gown of sea green gauze
that floated in panels as she moved, and should have looked

ridiculous on a woman of her age, yet somehow did not. It was cut very low in the bodice, which drew a frowning look from the duchess, together with a pungently voiced suggestion that a shawl of some kind would seem to be a necessity if she were not to take a severe chill.

The Glenvilles arrived on time, earning them the instant approval of Her Grace. They stood for a moment in the doorway, father and daughter making a handsome pair. Someone behind Serena drew in an audible breath, though she had no way of knowing if it was Cedric. She would not have blamed him, if it was.

Against her father's severe black and white, Melissa shimmered like a gossamer angel in a simple spangled white gown—the youthful epitome of lightness, innocence, and beauty—her hair confined by a simple white riband, a cluster of pale golden curls that immediately made Lady Charlotte's coiffure seem falsely gilded.

Seeing the dazed look in Cedric's eyes, Serena acknowledged defeat even as she smiled and walked forward to greet the guests and draw them into the room and toward their hostess.

"Well, Lionel, it's been a long time."

The duchess's booming voice broke the spell of silence. Sir Lionel bowed over her hand. "Too long, Elvira," he said easily. "But then, we both had our reasons. It is good to see you again. The years have treated you well."

"Have they, indeed?" she returned. "Well, as I remember, you were ever a flatterer."

Darcy, watching the little scene, was amused to note that Her Grace's brisk words belied her pleasure in the compliment—indeed, had it been anyone but the duchess, he might have sworn he detected a hint of coyness in her reaction.

"May I present my daughter?" Sir Lionel said with a

beaming smile. "Melissa, my love, come and make your curtsy."

"Very prettily done, my child," said the duchess. And to her father, "She's very like Marianne."

"Good of you to say so," he returned huskily. "I make no secret that she means everything to me. And that, in consequence, I can never hope to repay the service rendered to her some days ago by the duke and his fiancée."

"Well, I am sure Cedric don't consider you to be indebted to him." The duchess became brisk once more. "Cedric, do you and Miss Fairburn make Sir Lionel and his daughter known to everyone. Dinner will be served shortly."

The evening seemed incredibly long to Serena. Once dinner was over, and they repaired to the salon once more, a little entertainment was called for. She played the piano and sang a verse or two of a popular ballad, and then Melissa was persuaded by her father to sing for them, declaring that she had a very sweet voice.

"Don't be shy, puss," her father said encouragingly. "We are among friends, after all. Miss Fairburn has done her bit most charmingly and will, I am sure, accompany you if we ask her nicely."

"Yes, of course I will, if you will tell me what you would like to sing."

"And I'll turn the pages," Cedric volunteered with such alacrity that his mother stared.

"I hardly know . . ." Melissa's voice was diffident. "May I see what music there is?" Together the three young people pored over the sheets of music, heads close together. "Oh, you have some Mozart. I could manage 'Voi che sapete', I think. We performed selections from *The Marriage of Figaro* at school recently."

"That's the ticket," said her father, beaming. "You

should have seen my Melissa, Elvira, quite exceptional. Set everyone talking, as I remember."

"Papa!"

"Well, well, I'll not put you to the blush."

Charlotte put a hand to her mouth to stifle a yawn, and Eustace would have left the room, had his sister-in-law's beady eye not been fixed on him in warning. Darcy stared at the ceiling, as if in rapt contemplation of the music. Only Mr. Morville and the duchess—and Sir Lionel, of course—gave the young girl their full attention. Until she began to sing. And then everyone present realized that he had not been guilty of a father's exaggeration.

Her voice was a clear, light soprano, with just the right degree of mischievousness required of Cherubino—an enchanting performance.

It really wasn't fair, Serena thought, that any one person should have so many gifts, without at the same time, being thoroughly pert and unlikable. One couldn't even call her spoiled—a trifle precocious, perhaps, but that was not to be wondered at, with no mother to take her in hand, and a father who doted on her. But, for the most part, Miss Glenville behaved exactly as she should.

After the congratulations had died down, Miss Pennyweather played so that those who wished might stand up for a country dance. At first it seemed only the younger members of the party would do so. Then Sir Lionel took the initiative.

"Lady Charlotte," he pleaded with such gallantry and with such a twinkle in his eyes that she could not resist. "May I have the honor?"

Charlotte looked at him anew. Hubert was not at his best on the dance floor, and she had determined not to stand up. But Sir Lionel wore his years well and was not unattractive.

"Why not?" she said with a flutter of her long eyelashes.

Serena was not sure whether she should dance at all, given her present state of mourning, but the duchess waved away her reservations.

"To be sure, in a small informal family gathering such as we are at present, I believe such considerations need not concern you. Though, of course, it is very proper in you to put the matter forward."

She was pleased, for she loved to dance. Nevertheless, she had selflessly insisted that Cedric should partner their guest and regretted her generosity almost immediately as, out of the corner of her eye, she saw Mr. Morville moving relentlessly toward her. But in the nick of time she was claimed by Darcy.

"I had thought you would disdain such parochial pursuits," she said, not wishing to seem too eager.

But he had read her thoughts too well. "Would you rather be pawed by Mama's inamorato?" he murmured provocatively.

Serena half laughed and bit her lip. "You are very persuasive, my lord. How can I possibly resist?"

Darcy was an excellent dancer, which did not altogether surprise her. There was a litheness about him that made it difficult to imagine him capable of a clumsy action. What did surprise her, however, was the effect his closeness had upon her. Even his lightest touch seemed to burn through the silk of her gown, and she found herself irrationally wondering what it would be like to waltz with him.

"That is a remarkably pretty child," he said, breaking her mood. She glanced across to where Melissa and Cedric were performing the turning step of the dance. "Very little conversation, of course, but pretty enough to engage the interest of a susceptible young man, wouldn't you say?"

"If you are trying to be contentious, my lord, you will

not succeed. Cedric and I understand one another very well."

"Of course you do," he said smoothly. "It was merely a hypothetical observation."

As the figure of the dance separated them at that moment, she was obliged to subdue the lively retort she had been about to make, and by the time they came together again, she had thought better of it.

Sir Lionel and Melissa took their leave at ten o'clock in an atmosphere decidedly more harmonious than Masham Court was used to enjoy.

Chapter Thirteen

A very satisfactory evening," proclaimed the duchess as the family returned en masse from the obligatory Sunday morning service in the chapel, conducted by Mr. Clayton with commendable brevity. Only Darcy had dared to absent himself.

The chapel was situated at the far end of the east wing and entailed a considerable walk through endless corridors where the draughts seemed to gather on even the mildest of days. And on this day there was a decided chill of winter about it. But no one, even Eustace, had dared to absent themselves from this ritual gathering.

Charlotte teetering along, wearing the most inappropriate footwear, and wrapped to the ears in furs, was, to everyone's surprise, in a benevolent, even reminiscent mood.

"I can vividly remember how Papa made us sit through the most tedious hour-long sermons by his then cleric, Mr. Mayhew—a more egregious bore you could not imagine—and woe betide us if we nodded off." Her laugh trilled. "Sometimes, Eustace would deliberately make himself sick so that he didn't have to attend, even if it meant having to swallow one of nurse's disagreeable paregorics."

Eustace shuddered with distaste at the memory. "Anything was preferable to sitting shivering for hours while that man prosed on about the 'Fires of Hell'. I frequently found myself wishing that they might descend upon us in our supposed wickedness—at least a few flames would have warmed the place up a bit." His voice took on a vitriolic note. "I was once misguided enough to say as much and was beaten for my levity."

Cedric chuckled audibly, earning himself a repressive frown from his mother.

"So I should hope. Such frivolity must always be discouraged. One does not attend worship in order to be comfortable. I feel sure that Cedric's father never belittled his duty to his Maker."

"Well, that just shows how wrong you can be, Elvira. For I well remember a time—"

"Thank you, Charlotte," Her Grace interposed swiftly. "We have had enough tedious reminiscence for one morning."

Cedric choked back his merriment, and reached for Serena's hand as they hurried on ahead of the main party.

They reached the main hall to find Darcy engaged in conversation with Miss Glenville, who had that moment arrived in her father's carriage, accompanied by her maid. Her face was framed by the prettiest pale green bonnet, adorned with blond ribbons, and she wore a deeper green velvet pelisse that lent an added brilliance to the sparkle in her eyes.

"I hope you don't mind, Your Grace. Papa said it would be quite in order for me to drive over to thank you on his behalf for a very pleasant evening," she said with charming diffidence. "For myself, I have never enjoyed anything so much."

"Very prettily expressed sentiments," said the duchess approvingly. "What a pity you did not arrive a little sooner. You might then have accompanied us to chapel."

Miss Glenville tried valiantly to look disappointed and

was much relieved when Cedric braved his mother's frowns to say that she had missed nothing but a rather earnest sermon, followed by Miss Pennyweather's valiant attempts to coax a passable performance out of the ancient organ.

"Now, as it happens, you are just in time to join us in a little light refreshment," he said with an encouraging smile.

"Oh! You are very kind, Your Grace." The gold-tipped eyelashes fluttered nervously as Melissa blushed and confessed, "I had not intended . . . that is, Papa said I must not impose . . ."

"You do not impose," the duchess informed her graciously. "As my son informed you, we are about to repair to the Blue Drawing Room to partake of a light repast. I am sure you would not dislike a glass of cordial and a ratafia biscuit or two. Serena, I'm sure I may leave Miss Glenville in your charge." And she bowed her head and proceeded up the stairs.

"Well, this is splendid," Cedric said. "You have brightened up our morning no end. Isn't that so, Serena?"

With mixed feelings Serena stepped forward. "Yes, indeed. But do, pray, let us all go upstairs. This hall is incurably draughty."

Cedric took it upon himself to escort Melissa Glenville, so that Serena was left to follow in their wake. As she did so, she found Darcy watching the scene with a satirical eye. He fell into step beside her.

"Your forbearance fills me with unreserved admiration," he murmured so that only she could hear him. "I can think of few women among my acquaintance who, faced with a similar situation, would not be struggling with an overwhelming desire to scratch Miss Glenville's eyes out."

"Indeed? And what purpose would that serve, my lord?"

He chuckled in genuine amusement. "Oh, very little *pur-*

pose, to be sure, my dear, but only consider the satisfaction it must afford."

Serena half laughed and bit her lip. "Which would in turn be self-defeating by making one appear disagreeably selfish."

"You are either very wise, or very foolish," he said with a touch of asperity. "And I'm damned if I know which."

"That must indeed irritate you, my lord. For you are usually so decided in your opinions."

He looked for sarcasm, but the demure look she returned him had no obvious hidden barbs, and after a moment he gave her one of his half-angry looks and shook his head.

They had by now reached the drawing room, where Melissa was being urged by Cedric to take a seat close to the fire.

"And should you not remove your bonnet and pelisse?" he urged solicitously. "It would not do at all if you were to become overheated and take a chill when you leave."

"Well, perhaps. Just for a few moments. I did promise Papa that I would not stay . . ."

"And how is your father this morning?" Charlotte asked, at her most charming. "What a pity he could not accompany you. We did so enjoy his company last evening. Such a pleasure to converse with a gentleman so well versed in so many subjects."

Serena saw Lynton's eyebrows lift and feared some cutting rejoinder, but there was a diversion in the shape of Mr.Morville, who had been sent to bring Zoe to her mistress.

Mr. Morville had overheard the conversation, and jealousy rose like bile in his throat as he remembered how blatantly Charlotte had flirted—yes, there was no kinder word for it—she had flirted with Sir Lionel last evening, almost to the extent of cutting him out altogether.

The memory seared anew, making him squeeze the animal, and earning himself a peevish nip from her very sharp teeth, and causing him to bite back a decidedly ungentlemanlike curse as he churlishly thrust the pug at Charlotte.

"Oh, I did not know you had a dog, Lady Charlotte," Melissa exclaimed. "She seems a little nervous of company."

Melissa half put out her hand and was growled at for her pains, so that she spilled some cordial on her dress, and Cedric at once produced a large white handkerchief to mop it up, realized the impropriety of attempting to perform such a task himself, and handed it to Serena who proved more than competent.

"Zoe is nothing of the kind, poor dear," Lady Charlotte retorted, her gushing manner momentarily forgotten. "She simply dislikes the way Hubert holds her."

Melissa blushed and bit her lip. "I am sorry. I did not mean . . . I am not very used to small dogs, you see. We have a large, rather old retreiver at home, but he is the gentlest and friendliest of animals."

"There is no need to apologize, Miss Glenville," Cedric said swiftly, a view that was echoed by his mother.

"I have always maintained that the drawing room is not the place for dogs," the duchess said, directing a quelling glance at her sister-in-law.

Serena, stepping back to survey her handiwork, said practically, "There, I believe that has removed the worst of the stain. But when you return home, I should advise your maid to sponge it for you, just to be sure."

"Thank you. You are so kind!" Melissa murmured incoherently. "I think perhaps I had better go now. Papa will be wondering . . ."

"Quite so," said the duchess. "You may carry my good wishes to your father and inform him that you are both welcome at any time. And I hope that in future there will be no dogs to create mayhem," she concluded, casting a frigid look at Charlotte.

When all the good-byes had been said, Serena went with Cedric to see Melissa safely into her carriage, determined that her kindness should be imparital.

"And on your next visit, you must allow His Grace to show you some of his drawings of butterflies. I think you will like them." She felt rather than witnessed Cedric's reaction as she smiled and concluded resolutely, "They are very beautiful."

"Oh, I should like that!"

The carriage rolled away down the drive. "You didn't mind my mentioning your collection? Only Miss Glenville seems just the kind of young lady who would appreciate them."

He did not answer at once, and when he did, she was neither surprised nor cheered to hear him say abruptly, "Not precisely, though I would as soon you left me to decide such matters in future for myself."

That night sleep would not come.

Serena lay for what seemed like hours after Bessie had left her, listening to the rising wind that rattled the windowpanes and watching the candle flame leap, sending grotesque shadows across the ceiling.

Her thoughts were almost as uncontrolled as the weird shapes that gyrated around the room. She had become very fond of Cedric and knew that he returned her affection. But he had never looked at her as she had seen him look at Melissa Glenville, and a pain so real that she gasped at its ferocity pierced her as she knew that he, that no man would ever look at her that way.

For an instant a worm of jealousy threatened to sour her liking for the young girl, who could bring such a light into his eyes. But that would be both unfair and unjust, for Melissa had done nothing to encourage Cedric. It had happened like a lightning flash, and she told herself that it would die as quickly if not encouraged.

So why had she deliberately tried to throw them together? To tempt fate? Or was it sheer perversity?

Her mind continued to twist and turn. If it were simply a matter of her own happiness, would she end the betrothal and relinquish her chance of becoming Duchess of Cornwell with all the benefits that such rank entailed? Her innate honesty forced her to admit that she would be reluctant. She was growing daily more used to good living, to being waited on. Why should she give it all up for a pair of green eyes that had momentarily enslaved Cedric? And even if she were willing, it would not do. Her mother, her whole family were depending on her, and everything was arranged.

So engrossed in thought was Serena that she almost missed the sound of the horses. She was out of bed in a flash and at the window. The trees were lashing round in the wind, as uncontrolled as her own thoughts. The bare branches whipped back and forth, and at first it wasn't easy to pick out the riders. Then she saw them, but this time they were riding more slowly, and heading back toward the stables.

Quite suddenly, she could no longer bear not to know. She crossed to the cupboard and reached for her heavy black cloak, pulling it close around her. The house was silent, and every creak of the floorboards sounded like a pistol shot.

The passage leading to the muniments room was also the quickest way to the stables. In complete darkness Serena felt her way along to the outer door. The wind almost took it out of her hand, and she had the greatest difficulty closing it again.

Her eyes soon adjusted to the darkness as she ran toward the stables, and above the wind she heard the horsemen approaching. The second stall was empty, and soundlessly she raised the latch and stepped inside.

As she did so, a hand covered her mouth and she found herself being lifted off her feet.

Chapter Fourteen

The arm that imprisoned Serena, lifting her off her feet with ease, could only belong to one man. After the initial shock, she ceased to struggle and was not in the least surprised to hear a familiar voice in her ear.

"Not a sound if I release you. Do I have your word?"

She nodded vigorously, and a moment later Darcy removed his hand from her mouth and set her down, though his arm still confined her. She had bitten her tongue, but the faint jingle of a bridle took her mind off the pain and the taste of blood.

"What are you doing here?" she breathed.

"The same as you, I imagine," he murmured dryly, and laid a finger against her mouth as horses came nearer. "Hoping to waylay a phantom rider."

The door to the next stall opened, and a voice said quietly, "I'll see to Starlight, Y'r Grace. I reckon the sooner you're in bed, the better, beggin' Y'r Grace's pardon."

"Don't preach, Robbie, there's a good fellow."

"It's Cedric!"

Surprise made Serena incautious. She pulled away from Darcy and was into the next stall before he could prevent her.

"Serena! What in heaven's name are you doing here?" If

she had been surprised, Cedric was doubly so. He sounded like a guilty schoolboy, at once aggrieved and defensive.

"I daresay she might care to ask the same of you, my fine cousin," Darcy said, leaning nonchalantly on the swaying door.

"You, too? Oh, devil take it! Can I do nothing without being watched?"

"It would appear not. However, I confess I am intrigued. In fact, you might say that Serena and I have come quite independently to satisfy our curiosity."

For a moment Cedric stood, irresolute. Then he sighed, his shoulders appearing to sag a little, as if suddenly succumbing to weariness.

"We can't talk here. You had better come along to my rooms. Good night, Robbie. And thank you."

"Goodnight, Y'r Grace." The young man touched his forehead in salute.

They crossed the garden to the south terrace in silence and were presently entering his comfortable parlor where several lamps burned low. Cedric turned them up while Darcy threw off his topcoat and took a poker to the fire, before throwing on a couple of small logs.

Serena, suddenly very conscious that she was wearing nothing but her nightgown beneath her cloak, continued to hover in the shadows until Cedric urged her forward.

"Do sit down, my dear Serena." Cedric indicated a comfortable chair near the fire. "You must be chilled to the bone. I cannot apologize enough for all the trouble I seem to have inadvertently caused you."

She sat, being careful to draw the cloak tightly about her, blushing as Darcy's ironic smile convinced her he was aware of her embarrassment.

"Will Grove not hear us and come to investigate?"

"I think not," Cedric said with a confidence that puzzled

Serena. He opened a cupboard and took out a couple of wine bottles and several jars. "Why don't I make us some mulled wine? I'm quite an expert."

"Are you, by Gad! You seem to be an expert at quite a number of things, my fine young cousin." Darcy gently pushed Cedric into the chair beside Serena. "You sit down, and I'll mull the wine. You can scarcely stand on your feet."

Serena, too, had noticed Cedric's pallor, which the lamplight accentuated, gouging great hollows in his cheeks.

"Why do you do it, Ceddie?" she beseeched him. "Why do you sometimes drive yourself in a way so injurious to your health?"

He was silent for a moment, watching Darcy take the pan from the hook, draw the corks from the wine bottles, and assemble the sugar and spices.

"You can have no idea how frustrating it is to be constantly told what you cannot do—to be constantly denied pursuits most boys and young men take for granted."

Serena had occasionally sensed a kind of impatience in him, but now there was a bitterness in his voice she would never have expected.

"But why have you never said? You always seem so conciliatory—or almost always," she amended.

He sighed. "I long ago accepted that much would be denied me, and made a life for myself accordingly."

Darcy put the pan on the hob and settled into the chair opposite. "Your study of wildlife?"

"A nice innocent pastime that soon became more than just a hobby," Cedric agreed. "And I would not change that for anything. But occasionally there is a small devil inside me that demands to be satisfied."

"Oh, Ceddie, why did you not tell me?"

He smiled his lopsided smile and reached for her hand.

"My dear Serena, your coming has been one of the best things that has happened to me in a long time. You can have no idea what a difference it has made to my life. But why should I burden you with my quirks?"

"Because if I am to be your wife, I would like to know what makes you happy, or unhappy."

He made no immediate answer, but smoothed her hand with his thumb in an abstracted way.

"And so you go haring off across the fields like a madman to Jack Finchley's place at Mile End," Darcy concluded, breaking a silence that was pregnant with unspoken thoughts.

"You already knew that the mystery rider was Cedric!" Serena accused him.

"I had my suspicions. And I've had Jack keeping his eyes open ever since you confided in me. But nothing happened until this evening. He obeyed my instructions to follow Ceddie, then came back and told me where he had gone."

"The devil he did!" Cedric was on his feet. "It comes to something when you're spied on in your own house, and by the very people you thought you could trust!"

Darcy leaned forward and stirred the wine, seemingly unmoved by two pairs of accusing eyes. Then he reached for the poker and set it among the flames.

"Come down from the boughs, ungrateful wretch! You should thank heaven we were concerned for your safety." Without looking up, he added, "Perhaps you would care to taste this brew to see if it meets with your approval before I plunge the poker in? To prove that I have no ulterior motives, I am perfectly willing to try it first in order to assure you it isn't poisoned."

Cedric struggled with his feelings for a moment, then

grinned ruefully. "Idiot! It was you taught me to make it in the first place. There are some claret cups in the cupboard."

Serena sipped the wine warily at first. It slipped down in a very comfortable way.

"You need have no fears. I don't gamble seriously," Cedric said. "Not like Uncle Eustace or your mama. Picquet is my passion, but I never play for high stakes, or hardly ever. And I almost always win."

"Such complacence. I'll take you on some time—and then we shall see."

Serena found the talk of cards rather boring, but the wine was warming her quite wonderfully, and her mind began to wander so that she scarcely noticed as her half-empty glass was replenished.

"I still don't understand about Grove," she said aloud. "He guards you like a benevolent jailer."

Cedric's smile became a wicked grin, and already he was looking better as Darcy refilled their glasses.

"Poor old Grove. So conscientious. He does like his drop of brandy in warm milk at bedtime—and, when necessary, I simply add a few drops of the laudanum he's always pressing me to take." The grin became a chuckle. "He sleeps like a baby."

"Cedric!"

"Such depravity." Darcy mocked him. "But it won't do, you know. Serena may not be the only one to have observed your late night perambulations, so you will oblige me, us, by abandoning your adventures for the next few weeks—at least until after the wedding."

"But why? It hurts no one."

"Humor me."

"We don't want anything to happen to you."

Serena's tongue, loosened by the wine, let the words slip

out. Darcy frowned at her, and she smiled back, keeping her eyes open with an effort. He looked more closely at her.

"How much of this wine have you had?"

"Not a lot. It's lovely and warming, all the way down."

"Good God!" His laugh was abrupt. "Ceddie, I believe your wife-to-be is halfway disguised!"

"I am nothing of the kind," she protested. "I'm just a little sleepy."

"Then bed is the place for you, my girl."

She sat up, and the room spun and steadied. "I am not your girl."

"Nevertheless." He hauled her to her feet. "Which room are you in?"

"Oh, it's down a long passage . . . miles and miles down . . . "

He began to laugh. "Wretched girl. Do you know the room, Ceddie?"

"It's on the main corridor close to the west tower—the one Mother's sister, Maud, always used to have when she came years ago—before she popped her clogs."

"I know it. Come along, Serena." He hauled her unceremoniously to her feet and felt her sway. "Oh, good God, she's drunk as a wheelbarrow! You're going to have a terrible head in the morning."

"Hadn't I better come with you?" Cedric asked.

"No. You're better employed in removing all traces of our night of debauchery if you don't want Grove to twig and ring a peal over you—or, worse still, inform on you to your mama."

"Don't even think it!"

Serena was suddenly very tired and glad of Darcy's strong arms encircling her as he half supported, half carried her along a passage toward a pair of back stairs leading to the upper landing.

"Will your maid be waiting up for you?"

"Oh, no, she went to her bed hours ago . . ."

She would, he thought, and hoped to God no one saw them. Somewhere a clock chimed three. With luck everyone would be asleep by now. He found the room without too much difficulty. A candle still burned, but only just. It guttered in the draught as the door swung to, and for a moment he thought it would be extinguished. But it still flickered feebly. He sat Serena on the edge of the bed.

"Now, will you be all right?"

She nodded vigorously, swayed, and groaned. "My head is spinning."

He laughed softly. "Heaven help us if we are discovered now."

He stooped to remove her shoes and undo the clasp of her cloak, which immediately slid from her shoulders. As he lifted her to her feet and threw back the bedclothes, she swayed against him, and all desire to laugh left him, replaced by desire of a different kind. Her body was pliant, and through the cotton of her nightgown he could feel the softness of her, the swell of her breasts beneath his hands, the sweet curve of hip and thigh against his body. It would be so easy to take advantage—to plunder all that sweet innocence.

With his heart thudding in his chest, he lowered her to the bed and pulled the covers up round her.

"G'night," she sighed and was asleep.

Darcy stood for a long time, looking down at her in the flickering light, wondering what it was about her that set his pulse racing. She was not at all in his usual style, but there was an inner strength and courage that challenged his accepted view of women. Now sleep softened the contours of her face as she nestled into the pillow, lending a touch of vulnerability to that full lower lip. He touched the long plait of hair curving into the line of her neck and on impulse bent and touched his lips to hers. She sighed and seemed to smile.

Then he blew out the candle and felt his way to the door.

Serena finally came to herself to hear the wind howling round west tower in a most unfriendly way. Her head was aching, and she had a distinct feeling of being not quite the thing.

"I thought you was never going to wake up, Miss Serena, but I didn't like to disturb you—you looked as if you was dead to the world."

Gingerly, she sat up, and groaned, her mind still reluctant to remember why she felt so strange. "Bessie, do you think you could look in that small medicine chest. There should be some of James' powders . . . "

Bessie flung back the curtains and the late autumn sunlight, pale and painfully bright, filled the room. "Now I come to see you proper, you do look a bit green round the gills, as me mam used ter say . . . "

"Not now, Bessie. The powder, if you please. And, do pull that curtain to a trifle. The sun is almost directly in my eyes."

"I'm sorry, miss." The maid scuttled across the room to do as she was bid, found the powders, and came back with some water in a glass. "If it was anyone else, I'd say you'd had a drop over the odds last night. My brother—"

"Bessie!"

"Yes, miss. Sorry, miss." The girl blushed, tipped the powder into the glass, and stirred vigorously. "You'll not be wantin' to get up for a bit, I'm thinkin'," she said judiciously.

"What time is it?"

"Just gone nine, Miss Serena. But there's nobody gone

down to breakfast yet, as far as I know, savin' Her Grace an' that Miss Pennyweather, and the curate. A right jolly threesome ... " She saw her mistress frown and changed the subject. "Lord Lynton had his early and went out riding. Will I lay out your riding dress, Miss Serena?"

"No. Not this morning, Bessie. Perhaps later. I'll wear the brown woollen gown for now."

The mention of Lord Lynton brought back the events of last night, and their culmination ... Oh, dear God, had she dreamed it, or had he really brought her back here and ...? The blood flooded into her face so that it became impossible to complete the memory. She felt as if her whole body was aflame with embarrassment. Thank God Darcy had gone out. How could she ever look him in the face again?

Serena finally entered the breakfast room, pale, but composed. Only Mr. Morville was present, his shirt points supporting a face suffused with angry color.

He greeted her abruptly and told her that Sir Eustace was cutting short his stay. He had received a message to the effect that there were matters urgently requiring his attention.

"I had the intention of returning to town myself tomorrow, Miss Fairburn, but her ladyship informs me that she means to remain until the weekend. Sir Lionel, it seems, is to return Her Grace's hospitality. You are all invited, and he particularly wishes Lady Charlotte to be among his dinner guests." His breast swelled with indignation. "I am not included. An oversight, no doubt. I daresay he did not realize that she and I—but there it is. She is adamant that she must go."

Serena did not like Mr. Morville, but she did feel sorry for him. He had spared no pains in lavishing every luxury upon Darcy's mama, and she really did not treat him as she should.

"I daresay the matter can very easily be rectified," she

suggested soothingly. "Sir Lionel is a most accommodating gentleman—"

"No, no. That will not serve at all. One can only take so much. If she will not change her mind, I shall not wait until tomorrow. I shall leave today, and Charlotte may remain without the benefit of my company. Let her secretary fetch and carry for her—she pays him enough to do so. Or rather, I have done so, until now. But no more."

Oh dear. Jealousy had reared its head in no small fashion. Serena remembered how, on the previous morning, as she had passed the corridor where Mr. Bickerstaffe was housed on her way to take her early morning ride, she had glimpsed Lady Charlotte, very much *en deshabille*, disappearing into her secretary's room—one could not mistake those draperies. And she had wondered what could possibly be taking her ladyship there at such an hour.

If Mr. Morville had witnessed a similar indiscretion, Serena very much feared that Lady Charlotte was about to lose her provider. It would be no wonder if the poor man had grown tired of being put upon; the wonder was rather that he had put up with her quirks for so long.

It occurred to Serena, as she walked in the garden after breakfast in the hope of clearing a lingering woolliness in her head, that if Mr. Morville did leave Lady Charlotte, Darcy would once more be obliged to support his mama. And, it seemed, her secretary. He would not like that one little bit.

Perhaps Lady Charlotte hoped to ensnare Sir Lionel. He had certainly eyed her with some interest, but from all Serena had gleaned, though he might contemplate a little harmless dalliance, he had loved Melissa's mother too much to ever wish to replace her.

A dog yapping brought her back to the present. She saw Mr. Bickerstaffe approaching, walking Zoe, or, more accurately, he was being dragged along as an unwilling companion. He was a tall, thin young man dressed in sober black—no more than thirty, probably less—with a tense, sharp-featured face that had an almost unnatural pallor.

"Good morning," she said as they drew close. "I see you have acquired an extra duty. I do not envy you."

He touched his hat. "Sometimes, one does not have a choice." His face gave little away, but she felt a deep bitterness in him that compelled her to speak.

"I suppose not. It cannot be easy for you. I mean . . . that is . . . " She knew she should never have started, but it was too late to draw back now. "I know a little of your background. And I understand, though my own case is not comparable with yours. It must be galling to be obliged to take orders where you were once used to give them."

She was by now wishing with all her heart that she had not begun, but he seemed almost indifferent to her embarrassment.

"One must live," he said abruptly as Zoe pulled at the lead, and this time there was no mistaking the bitterness. "It is ironic, is it not? My great, great grandfather was knighted for services to the crown; since then our family has maintained its unswerving loyalty. Now, charlatans have cheated my father out of every penny he possessed, and no one, let alone the crown, lifts a finger to help him."

She could think of nothing to say, nor did he seem to expect her to speak.

"Do not waste your pity, Miss Fairburn," he said harshly as he touched his hat again. "I do not mean to walk dogs forever."

She watched him go, his thin figure being jerked by the uncontrollable Zoe. To be sure, he was not a very likable young man upon first acquaintance, but he had been quite wretchedly ill-used by fate.

And although their situations were not dissimilar in some respects, she had the advantage and support of a loving family and had been granted the great good fortune of improving her lot. Whereas he had nothing, not even hope.

Chapter Fifteen

Serena had come round by way of the orchard where, among the leaves swirled by the wind, there were still a few fallen apples for Smoke's morning treat.

She was surprised to find Sir Eustace in the stable yard, dressed for riding and giving orders to his coachman.

"I leave at noon, Hudson, so you will have the coach on the forecourt by eleven-thirty."

"Yes, m'lord."

Serena did not really wish to meet him, but one of the grooms had already seen her and wished her good morning.

Sir Eustace turned and greeted her abruptly.

"You are leaving us, I believe, sir?"

"I am. The country is devilish dull, don't y'know, especially in winter. And there are urgent matters awaiting my attention in town."

"But you will return, I hope, for the wedding?"

Serena hoped nothing of the kind, but politeness seemed to demand that she make the gesture. His reply was non-committal, featuring much complaint about the possibility of inclement weather and the "demned draughts." He hailed Cedric's groom, who was busy cleaning out Starlight's stall.

"I want a horse to take me to the village. That hack of my nephew's will do me well enough."

"Well, I'm not sure as His Grace . . . " Robbie Gibson was clearly embarrassed. "That is, supposing he was to be wanting Starlight himself, m'lord? There's several other good mounts as would carry y'r lordship . . ."

But Sir Eustace was not a man to be crossed, as Serena could have told him. It simply made him more stubborn.

"Damn your impertinence, boy! Do as you're told and saddle the brute up this minute!"

The young groom flushed up, and his mouth took on a stubborn line. Serena judged it to be time to intervene.

"Do as his lordship says, Robbie. I will vouchsafe to explain to His Grace, should he wish to ride"—her eyes met Robbie's—"though I doubt he will be abroad very early this morning."

He flushed, remembering their adventure of the previous night. Also, he was aware that all the other grooms were listening, and if Mr. Hurly, the head groom, should happen along, he'd be for it. "Well, if you say so, Miss Serena." He went reluctantly to saddle Starlight.

"Demned insolence! Servants questioning their betters. I wouldn't tolerate it!"

"Robbie Gibson is very protective of His Grace," Serena explained placatingly. "And it is true that Cedric is not keen to let anyone else ride Starlight."

"Well, I hope that he, at least, realizes that his uncle is not just anyone!"

The horse was presently led out, and Sir Eustace swung up into the saddle with an agility that surprised everyone and rode away without a word.

"His lordship rides well, I'll say that for him," Robbie admitted grudgingly.

Serena laughed and went on to where Smoke already had her head out, watching for her.

"I confess that I shall not be sorry to see Eustace leave,"

said the duchess, meeting Serena on her return to the house. "He was never an easy man, and age has not mellowed him."

"I believe Lady Charlotte is staying on."

"Silly woman!" Her Grace exclaimed impatiently. "At least she has given that creature, Morville, his congé—odious little parvenu! Though who will fund her excesses now remains to be seen. But that is for Darcy to worry about. I cannot hold myself responsible. I only hope she don't mean to make a-cake of herself over Sir Lionel, for I am convinced he sees her only as an amusing diversion."

Serena wondered how she should reply, but was spared the necessity as Her Grace was already off on another tack.

"I have not seen Cedric this morning. I hope he may not have taken one of his chills. This treacherous weather is always a source of worry. Affects his breathing, you know. Perhaps I should send Westerby to ascertain that all is well."

"I'm sure such a course is not necessary, Your Grace. In fact,"—the lie came out so smoothly that even Abby would have been deceived—"I believe I saw Darcy entering his rooms not above half an hour ago, so they are probably enjoying a comfortable gossip."

"Oh, well, if that is the case, we may expect them to be some time. Though I do feel he should be present to bid his uncle good-bye."

Mr. Morville had already departed, and only Serena was present to see him leave. He was accorded every civility by Westerby, but there was no sense of anyone caring whether he stayed or went.

"I wish you a safe journey, sir," Serena said, finding something rather touching in the lonely figure, made more marked by his ludicrous appearance and his attempt to

carry the moment off with a hauteur that in him scarcely
rose above pomposity.

Cedric did not put in an appearance until Sir Eustace's
coach was already at the door, which was thrown wide, allowing the cutting wind to send constant flurries of leaves
into the vestibule. He seemed quieter than usual, but was
apparently none the worse for his late night.

Westerby saw him and left his task of supervising the
disposal of Sir Eustace's baggage amidst a great bustle of
activity that contrasted quite markedly with Mr. Morville's
earlier departure. His expression betrayed a glimmer of
concern.

"Your Grace, I do not wish to arouse unnecessary alarm,
but his lordship's coach is almost completely loaded, and
there is no sign of him anywhere, not in his bedchamber or
the library . . ."

"But he must surely have returned by now." Serena
spoke impulsively and then realized they were all looking
at her. "His lordship came to the stables a good hour since
to borrow a horse in order to ride to the village," she explained, paused, glanced at Cedric, and concluded reluctantly, "He took Starlight and vowed he would not be gone
long."

"Starlight!" Cedric snapped the name out. "How dare
he . . . Robbie knows I allow no one—"

"It could not be helped, Cedric. Your uncle was most insistent, and Robbie was scarcely in any position to deny
him."

"No, of course not." He turned swiftly to apologize, but
his eyes were still troubled. "But an hour—one could walk
to the village and back in less time. Something must have
happened." He turned to Westerby. "A party must be sent
to look for them."

"No need." Darcy's voice broke in on him. "Our esteemed uncle is limping up the drive this very minute—"

"Limping?" Cedric started forward. "Where is Starlight? If he has . . ."

"Easy, Cedric." Darcy took his arm. "The horse isn't with him, but there's no reason to think the worst. Could have thrown him and galloped off."

"What is this?" demanded the duchess, who had arrived on the scene, prepared to accord her brother-in-law every last politeness. "Why is everyone standing in the hall with the door standing wide to every wind that blows? It will be wonderful, I'm sure, if we do not all take a chill!" Her voice rose in alarm. "Cedric, where are you going? Come back this instant! Only consider your chest, you cannot go out there without your cloak. Westerby, what are you about, allowing your master go unprotected into the cold?"

Serena had never seen Westerby so discomposed. "Forgive me, Your Grace, but His Grace has gone to meet Sir Eustace, who would appear to have suffered some kind of mishap."

"Mishap! What kind of mishap, pray?" Imperiously, with skirts crackling, she pushed her way through the servants who had gathered in the doorway to watch his lordship's approach. Her voice rose ominously. "Back to your duties this instant. Eustace, whatever have you been about?"

Sir Eustace had that moment arrived at the courtyard. His exquisite clothes were dirty and disheveled, the wig that so artfully concealed his balding head was wildly askew, and he was almost apoplectic with rage.

"Uncle Eustace?" Cedric intercepted his progress, standing before him like an inquisitor. "What have you done with my horse?"

"What have *I* done with . . . ?" Eustace ground the words out. "That's rich! It's what your cursed horse has done to me! He only dropped me in the middle of a cursed field and ran off. Demned saddle slipped—that incompetent fool of a groom obviously didn't tighten the girth properly."

"The devil!" Cedric exclaimed. "I must go to the stables at once to see if Starlight has returned! He may be hurt!"

"Damn! Don't trouble to ask if *I* am hurt! I'm only y'r own flesh and blood!"

Darcy, noting his lordship's reaction with narrowed eyes, thought it a fine performance. A little overdramatic, perhaps, which raised all kinds of interesting possibilities. He glanced quizzically at Cedric, who had the grace to look ashamed.

"I'm sorry, Uncle Eustace. I didn't mean to sound unsympathetic. But Robbie's a good groom. He wouldn't—"

"Oh, get along with you. I can't do with sanctimonious claptrap!"

Cedric bit his lip, hesitating. Serena made up his mind for him.

"Yes, do go along, Ceddie. You will not be at ease until you know that Starlight is safe. But don't rush, I beg of you." Then, turning to Sir Eustace, she asked quietly, "Are you indeed hurt, my lord?"

"Well, of course I'm hurt, madam! Sprained m'demned ankle, I shouldn't wonder!"

"Then let me summon a couple of footmen to help you to the library. You will be more comfortable sitting down. And perhaps a doctor should be sent for to take a look at your ankle." She turned to the duchess. "Ma'am?"

"Yes, yes, of course," the dowager said gruffly. "I hope I am not insensitive. Westerby, send one of the servants for Dr. Handley at once."

"Don't trouble yourself, Elvira. I want no sawbones poking and prodding at me." Eustace glared at the two footmen holding him up. "Where is Humbert? He's never there

when he's wanted! If he wasn't such a good valet,
I'd ... Humbert!"

"Coming, my lord!"

"He'll know what to do. A touch of arnica, some firm
bandaging, and a stiff brandy, and I'll be ready to leave."
His voice rose irascibly. "Ah, Humbert, about time!"

"Whatever is happening?" Charlotte, drawn by the com-
motion, came drifting down the stair.

Serena explained briefly what had happened.

"Oh, is that all? I quite thought some great tradegy was
being enacted. Eustace was ever a baby when he was hurt."

Darcy came up behind Cedric and took his arm.

"Easy does it, m'boy."

"I'm perfectly all right." His pace never altered.

"Ah, now there I beg to differ, Ceddie. You are already
out of breath."

Cedric knew his cousin was right, but it didn't quell the
feeling of impotent anger rising up in him. "Uncle Eustace
had no right to take Starlight! Saddle slipped, indeed! More
likely he rode him too hard!"

"That could well be the case. But don't, I beg of you,
take out your frustration on poor Robbie Gibson, or he will
blame himself."

It came as a great relief to find the horse back in the stable. Robbie was busy rubbing him down, and he seemed no
worse for his adventure.

"I didn't want to let him go, Your Grace, but Sir Eustace
wouldn't take no, and I—"

"It wasn't your fault, Robbie," Cedric assured him. "I
know how it is with my uncle when he's in that mood. And
at least the horse is all right."

"But I don't understand what happened, Your Grace. I
saddled Starlight proper, for all that his lordship was so im-

patient. I check the tack most particular every single day, as Your Grace knows."

"Yes, of course I know. You are most conscientious."

"So there shouldn't have been any problem. Yet one of the buckles was torn right off."

Darcy lent half an ear to the impassioned explanations, but he was in fact rather more interested in the saddle, which had been slung over the door, and which his own groom was presently examining.

"Anything interesting, Grayson?" he asked casually.

"Well, one of the girth buckles has gone, that's for sure, strap and all. And the other's badly twisted with the pressure that's been put on it." He peered closer. "Ah," he murmured. "Well, now, will you take a close look at that, m'lord."

Darcy held the girth up to the light. "What am I looking for?"

"There, see? Just where the strap's been ripped off. Someone's been a mite careless, wouldn't you say?"

It wasn't easy to spot until the light fell on it, but just at the point where the straps joined the girth, there were several faint marks—the kind of marks that could have been made by a sharp blade.

"So, you think the stitching was cut partway through?"

"I'd lay odds on it, m'lord."

"So would I, Grayson," Darcy murmured. "So would I. Very clever. It would hold for a while, but sooner or later, the thing would snap . . ."

"And no one would ever suppose it to be anything but an accident," Grayson agreed, his expression sober.

"This needs some thinking about," Darcy said grimly. "Meanwhile, the duke must know nothing. And not a word to young Robbie, either. I doubt he'll spot these marks, but then he wouldn't know what he was looking for."

"Which is, m'lord?"

"Malicious intent, Grayson. Someone with murder in mind planned this accident very cleverly. But, unless I'm mistaken, Sir Eustace wasn't the intended victim."

Grayson stared. "But who'd want to harm the duke, m'lord?"

"Gently, man." Darcy's glance strayed to his cousin, who was still in earnest conversation with Robbie. "We don't want to start any hares. I can think of several people who might have murder in mind, though I had hoped I was wrong. Remember that incident at the Crossed Keys a month or two back. I had my doubts then. Now it seems I was right and that we will need to keep a particular eye on His Grace for the next week or two, at least."

"That shouldn't be too difficult."

"Also, I would prefer that he know nothing about it. I doubt if I can dissuade him from riding, which might be a problem. Gibson is a good lad, but whether he is up to protecting my cousin is a different matter." He turned back to Grayson. "It may be that we shall have to do something about that."

Chapter Sixteen

With less than four weeks to go, the wedding plans were now well in hand. The duchess's dressmaker was in residence, with her sewing maid, and both were fully occupied. Several new gowns were already finished, and a new riding habit was in hand, made of wine velvet, braided in black, that would be very fine. The most vexing question, that of the wedding gown itself, had that day been decided. It was to be of pale gray heavy silk, the brief bodice embroidered with tiny beads.

"White is, of course, out of the question," the duchess had pronounced. "But gray or lilac would be quite acceptable, I believe. After all, with the exception of the Glenvilles, we shall be mostly family."

It had not originally been any part of Serena's plans to invite Sir Lionel and Melissa. But neither parent, it seemed, had noticed what was as plain as a pikestaff to her—namely that what she had prayed would be mere infatuation between Cedric and Melissa showed no sign of abating.

Cedric was better at disguising his feelings. If anything, his feelings for Melissa made him more than usually kind and attentive to Serena, but she was not fooled. She had tried several times to broach the subject, only to have him turn it deftly aside.

The dinner to which Sir Lionel had invited them at the

beginning of November had been torture for her. Melissa, in white gauze sprinkled with silver stars, had been heartbreakingly beautiful. She had been very bright and talkative, but her green eyes seemed huge in her little pointed face as she watched every move Cedric made.

And Darcy watched Serena, who was quite unaware of how much her eyes also betrayed her.

The older members of the party were too busy talking to notice anything untoward. The duchess's voice was frequently to be heard above the rest as she applied herself to the very excellent fare provided by her host's cook, being well past the age when one was required to toy with one's food as if it was of no concern. And Sir Lionel, being a courteous host, was happy to listen, as was his friend, Viscount Lonsdale, whom he had invited to stay.

The viscount was the best kind of dinner guest, with a ready flow of conversation and a fund of humorous anecdotes. But his greatest asset in Charlotte's estimation was that at two and forty, he was still a bachelor. How this came to be when he was quite obviously not impervious to a lady's charms, she could not imagine.

It would be rather splendid, she thought, if he and Sir Lionel were to vie for her favors. But their host seemed equally benevolent to all, and suddenly he became a trifle staid in her eyes, and she resolved to devote herself wholly to engaging his lordship's interest.

In other circumstances Serena might have enjoyed the charade, for there were moments when she suspected that Sir Lionel had invited the viscount precisely with Lady Charlotte in mind. But again and again, her eyes were drawn back to Melissa.

"Will she have him, do you think?" Darcy had murmured in her ear later in the comfortable drawing room.

She had been standing a little apart from the others,

watching Lady Charlotte flirting outrageously with the viscount, but just as Darcy spoke, she had seen, out of the corner of her eye, Melissa holding up a small china bird for Cedric's inspection. She was smiling, and there was an intimacy between them that brought a lump to her throat.

"It is not possible," she had murmured huskily, and he saw that they were talking at cross purposes.

Back at Masham he had drawn her aside into a small anteroom off the hall while everyone else moved toward the staircase, saving Cedric, who had slipped away to his own rooms without a word.

"What do you intend to do?" Darcy asked abruptly.

"I have no idea what you mean," she said, attempting to leave.

"Yes, you do." He put out a hand to detain her, and his fingers burned her skin. "You just won't admit you have a problem. Those two are eating their hearts out."

"It will pass," she said desperately.

His fingers had tightened. "And what if it does not?"

Serena thought of her family, of the duchess's wrath, should all her plans be disrupted. Her throat was constricted, and a great pain seemed to fill her chest.

"Cedric has honored me by asking me to marry him. He will not break that promise."

"Of course he won't, even if it means making the supreme sacrifice."

"You are being melodramatic, my lord! Please let me go!"

His fingers tightened. "You don't love him."

"I am very fond of him."

"Fond!" He almost spat the word out. "Is that all you ask of a man—to be fond of you?"

And before she knew what he was about, he had pulled her roughly to him, and his mouth came down on hers with a fierce intensity that drove all sense from her, her struggles ceasing almost before they had begun. It was as if her whole body was on fire, and she could not get enough of him. Gradually, his kisses gentled, trailing down to the pulse beating madly in her neck, his lips murmuring her name against her throat.

At last she found the strength to pull away.

His eyes glittered darkly in the half light. "Will Cedric ever make you feel like that?" he asked huskily.

"No," she admitted, her voice trembling. "But it changes nothing. We were speaking of marriage, not simply . . ." She could not frame the word.

He set her away from him. "So I was right in the first place." His voice had grown unbelievably cold. "You are determined to be a duchess, after all."

And he strode away before she could answer. Not that she had been capable of answering. And since that night, he had appeared only briefly, having expressed his intention of returning home to Ashford House.

Serena missed him more than she would have believed possible, for although he drove over most days to see his cousin, he very seldom stayed to dine.

Serena's resolution had hardened, and she picked up her life as though nothing had happened. For nothing really had, she told herself. Cedric was a little quieter than usual, but his attitude toward her did not change. And when he and Melissa met, they behaved with a touching propriety.

She knew nothing of the small scene that had been enacted shortly after that dinner party when he had gone alone to Melissa's home on a fine afternoon while Serena was busy with fittings for her trousseau, and had been permitted to take Melissa riding.

They had ridden in silence for a short distance before

dismounting beside a trickling stream that bordered the Cornwell estates on one side, then walking hand in hand along its edge.

"I don't know how I am to live without you," he said thickly. "I never dreamed that I could feel so . . . so tenderly, so completely for anyone as I do for you."

"Or I for you!" she confessed on a sob.

"If it were anyone but Serena, I could perhaps speak out. But I am very fond of her, and she has been so splendid, so supportive. Besides which—"

"No, no, you cannot desert her!" Melissa cried. "I would not permit it! If she were less kind, less generous . . . but I could not be happy, knowing how much she depends upon you."

"How dear you are!" He turned and took her in his arms, kissed her sweet lips, and felt them tremble. "But it is hopeless, I know that, for even if Serena agreed, I fear Mama would not. She would think you too young, too untried, to make me a suitable wife . . ."

"And Papa, much as he loves me, would be bound to agree with her! Oh, Cedric, how can life be so cruel? What are we to do?" Her head was on his shoulder, her fingers clutching at the cape of his coat while he soothed her with soft words. At last she raised her head, and her green eyes were drowning in unshed tears.

"W-We must be sensible, dearest one. I shall pretend that I am ill, so as not to attend your w-wedding! And in the s-spring we shall be going away to London. Perhaps it will be easier if we do not m-meet . . ."

Cedric took out a handkerchief and dried her lovely eyes. "You are so brave, my dear one!"

"Oh, no! I am not brave at all! But I must think what is best for you, and Serena is just the kind of wife you need—"

Here he put a hand over her mouth so that she could not continue.

"No, you are the wife I need! When I am with you, I forget my stupid weakness because you make me feel like a man—you make me feel strong!"

There seemed to be little else to be said, but they lingered for a long time, holding hands.

Mrs. Fairburn's weekly letter arrived, informing Serena that, in the event of nothing happening to detain them, the family would be ready to leave on the first day of December, it having been decided that the children would benefit from a few days in which to accustom themselves to their surroundings.

"Dear Connaught may be a few days late arriving—the dear boy is constantly at the duke's beck and call—but he vows he will arrive in good time for the *great day!*"

Abby's accompanying letter was full of all the small details that Mrs. Fairburn's overlooked, and Emily and the children added their own messages. Suddenly, Serena could not wait to see them all.

Lady Charlotte, meanwhile, was in her element. Viscount Lonsdale called daily to take her for a drive in his very handsome phaeton, and she was soon addressing him as Marcus.

"It's 'Marcus says this' and 'Marcus thinks that'," the duchess snapped one afternoon in exasperation. "One would suppose she was some gel of fifteen, instead of fast approaching five and forty! I find the whole thing most distasteful!"

"Lonsdale must enjoy her company," Cedric reasoned earnestly, his understanding heightened by his own frustrated love. "He would not otherwise be so often in her company. He doesn't even mind the pug, most of the time."

"Oh, your aunt knows how to charm a man, I'll give her that. But holding them is a different matter. Sooner or later, she becomes too demanding."

Julian Bickerstaffe's argument took the opposite line, for the more she was with the viscount, the less were her demands upon him, and, with too little to do, he was frequently to be found wandering about the place, looking disgruntled. Once Serena overheard them quarreling.

"Dear boy," she heard Lady Charlotte say in a disturbingly familiar way, "you must be patient. Of course I value you! How could it be otherwise? But I need someone to buy me pretty gew-gaws now that Hubert is gone. I have scarcely a penny to bless myself with, and Darcy is so penny-pinching, I vow I cannot bring myself to ask him for money!"

This brought an agonized "Oh, if only I were not so hamstrung! I would give you so much!" followed by soothing noises from Lady Charlotte, and then silence.

The conversation embarrassed Serena, for she felt she ought not to have listened. Darcy's mother could so easily manipulate people that one felt one should not like her—and yet, she could be quite charming.

There was a light fall of snow at the end of November, followed by a sharp frost. Serena hoped it would not persist. Mama would be very loath to travel in such inclement weather.

"You will not think of riding in this weather, surely?" Serena asked of Cedric, seeing that he was wearing his riding breeches and coat when they met over a late breakfast.

"Not unless the ground improves considerably," he assured her. "But I thought I might walk over to the stables later to see Starlight."

"Oh, do you think you should?" she said impulsively, thinking of its effect on his breathing. But she wished she had not spoken as his mouth tightened. "I'm sorry, Cedric. It was just . . . You must do as you please, of course. To be sure, it is not so very far from your rooms to the stables. I will come with you if you like."

"I advise you to wrap up very well if you do go out, Your Grace," said Mr. Bickerstaffe, who had been silently applying himself to a dish of ham and eggs. Ignoring Cedric's frown, he continued, "I took the dog out earlier, just for a short run, and the cold cut right through my coat. Of course, it is rather threadbare . . ."

His voice trailed off as Cedric frowned at him.

The frown was not intended as a rebuke, but rather as a measure of Cedric's concern that any man in his household, whether it be his responsibility or not, should want for a warm coat. But his quiet suggestion that something better could surely be found for him, and that he would put the matter to Grove, met with an abrupt rejection bordering on rudeness.

Cedric's look of mild surprise made Mr. Bickerstaffe blush painfully. "Forgive me, that was ungracious, I know. I am not yet used to . . . to accepting charity, though I know you had no such intention." He threw down his napkin, rose, bowed, and almost ran from the room.

In the silence left behind, Serena said quickly, "Poor man. It cannot be easy for him. I only wish I could like him more."

They did go to the stables in the end, both wrapped in dark heavy cloaks, their faces protected with scarves, which provided much occasion for merriment.

"I trust Hurly won't take us for a pair of villains." Cedric chuckled. "I don't fancy looking down the barrel of a shotgun."

This air of camaraderie went a long way to restoring to their relationship the kind of harmony it had lately lacked, and the reception they were accorded by their respective four-legged friends left them in high good humor.

In spite of the cold the sun shone brilliantly, making the whole countryside sparkle, so that they decided to take the longer route home via the small copse behind the stables, leading to the terraced gardens.

"Keep to the main path," Cedric said. "Palfry will have traps laid in the undergrowth."

It was good to see him so happy. Serena had been half wondering whether to broach the subject of Melissa, but now he was so much like his old self that she was loath to disrupt the harmonious mood. Also, she was again made aware of how much she was coming to appreciate this new way of life.

The copse was busy with small creatures going about their business. Wood pigeons cooed above their heads, and an occasional scuffle in the undergrowth betrayed the presence of rabbits.

"Lucky bunnies!" Cedric said, laughing as a tuft of a white tail vanished beneath a tangle of roots. "If Darcy had been with us, he would undoubtedly have come armed with a gun."

The words were hardly out when Serena heard the sudden snap of a twig, sounding remarkably like a gunshot, which made her look up. Sunlight slanting through the trees almost into her eyes also exposed the dull gleam of a gun barrel protruding from behind a tree trunk and aimed directly at them. She shouted a warning to Cedric, and acting more from instinct than conscious thought, pushed him aside with all her strength, landing on top of him as the sound of the shot filled the silence. Birds flew shrieking and flapping into the sky, and something red-hot seared through her outstretched arm.

The silence that followed seemed to stretch forever.

When Serena could bring herself to move, she sat up, the knowledge that she was still in one piece at first overriding the burning sensation in her arm. Her eyes scanned every tree trunk for some hint of a presence, but whoever had fired the gun had vanished without trace. Now her greatest concern was for Cedric, who still had not moved.

Panic was already rising in her, when, to her immense relief, he groaned and sat up.

"Are you all right?" she demanded urgently. "You aren't hurt?"

He sat with his arms on his knees, heaving for breath. "Just a bit winded. What happened?"

"Some maniac with a gun," she said shakily. "He seemed to be pointing it straight at us. I thought he meant to kill you."

Cedric looked at her long and hard. "So I owe you my life."

"I don't know about that. Everything happened so quickly . . ." Belated reaction hit her, making her head spin, and for a moment she bent forward and shut her eyes.

"Serena?"

"I'm all right. A slight dizziness, that's all. Delayed reaction." This wasn't quite all, for by now she had become aware of a burning pain in her arm. But she was fairly certain it was no more than a graze, and there was no point in upsetting Cedric further. She looked up and smiled a trifle tremulously. "No harm done. It was probably poachers trying for those wood pigeons."

For answer Cedric took hold of her cloak, which had a distinct double hole ripped in it. "Shot wouldn't make holes like that. I'll need to have a word with Palfry—get his keepers to keep their eyes open. I doubt it was one of them. They are forbidden to use guns so near the house. But we'll say nothing to my mother I think; you know what a drama

she makes of everything. Grove doesn't need to know, either. He's such an old woman."

"Only because he cares. But if that's what you want, I'll
walk round to the front, for he's sure to spot the rip in my
cloak and ask questions."

Serena kissed Cedric's cheek lightly and left him. She
was rather more shaken than she would admit, but the fresh
air soon made her feel better. It was disconcerting, however, to see Darcy's curricle drawn up in the courtyard, the
horses enveloped in a gentle cloud of steam. She would
have turned and retreated but Jack had already seen her.

"Mornin', miss," he called out, and Darcy, about to
mount the steps, turned and waited.

It was not his first visit since their quarrel, but she had so
far managed to avoid being alone with him. It was an awkward moment, but though his expression gave little away,
he seemed unaware of any awkwardness.

"You are not afraid to brave the elements, I see."

"On the contrary," she returned lightly. "I find this kind
of weather invigorating. Cedric and I have been round to
the stables."

"Whence Jack is bound. Off you go, lad. We don't want
them hanging about in the cold. And take them gently."

"Right'o, Guv."

The boy led the horses away, and Serena was left alone
with Darcy. As she approached the steps, she found herself
coming under intense scrutiny.

"You have caught your cloak on something," he observed as she drew near.

"It is nothing. I tore it on a bush. Bessie will mend it in a
trice."

Subconsciously, she heard Cedric's voice: *If Darcy had
been with us, he would undoubtedly come armed with a
gun.* The thought was dismissed almost before it took

shape—Darcy would never wish to harm Cedric—but it left an awkwardness in her manner, an awkwardness that his closeness did little to ease. Instead of letting her pass, he stretched out a hand to stay her. He gathered the cloak up with his free hand, looked closely at it, and lifted it to his nostrils.

"A tear, you say?" His voice had the oddest note to it. "I have yet to hear of a tear producing scorch marks, Serena."

Chapter Seventeen

I t is nothing, the merest graze!"
They were in the library, where a log fire burned bright.
Darcy had behaved in the most high-handed manner, marching her past the footman on the door and Westerby who happened to be in the main hall, and removing her cloak the moment the door was closed.

"You call this nothing."

He had pushed her unceremoniously into a chair, where he tore back the singed sleeve of her dress to reveal a long angry-looking scar. Looming over her, he demanded an explanation, the gist of which had done nothing to improve his temper.

"And supposing you had reacted less swiftly? You would almost certainly have been killed!"

"Well, I wasn't. Nor was Cedric," she returned, incensed. "I don't understand why you are so out-of-reason-cross!"

"You know why," he said tersely. "Now, tell me again exactly what happened. Think back carefully."

"I am doing, but it all happened so quickly. We were talking, and I just turned and saw something—the sunlight touching the barrel of a gun—a kind of shape behind it . . . a figure, I suppose. I dragged Cedric to the ground just as the gun went off. Darcy, do you think someone is trying to kill Cedric?"

"I don't know," he said unconvincingly.

"But that's terrible! Who would want—?"

"What happened afterward?"

"Nothing! By the time we had drawn breath, there was nothing, not even a sound. Now, will you please stop interrogating me!"

To her horror she was trembling and tears of weakness threatened. Seeing her distress at last, he drew a breath and went across to the sideboard, coming back with a glass of brandy.

"Drink this," he said tersely.

Serena blinked, eyeing it with distaste. "I don't need it."

"Drink it."

"You drink it," she retorted, some of her spirit returning. "It might make you better tempered. I can explain away a grazed arm, but the servants will be shocked to the core if they smell brandy on my breath at this hour of the morning."

Darcy choked on a sound that was half laughter, half exasperation, and tossed back the brandy in one gulp.

"You are a very stubborn, self-opinionated young woman, do you know that? At this moment I don't know whether to kiss you or strangle you. I must be crazy to love you!"

For a moment the words didn't register. When they did, her confusion mounted. "But you don't! You can't!"

He watched her myriad expressions with interest, one eyebrow quirked. "I thought I had made my feelings very plain last week."

Serena blushed scarlet at the memory. "But that was . . . . simply an attempt to make me change my mind about Ceddie!"

"True. And why should I want you to do that? I am fond of Cedric, but there are limits to what one will do for one's cousin."

"We are forever coming to cuffs! You know we are!" She was gabbling now. "And I am not in the least pretty, or eligible . . . or anything . . . "

"The first two I will accept, but I dispute the 'anything'."

He was laughing at her. But it was the laughter of love, and at last she began to believe him. "Oh, what a coil!"

Darcy lifted her bodily from the chair as if she were a mere featherweight, and she sighed with delight, for it was the dream she had thought would never come true.

"Nothing is impossible if you want it enough," he murmured, his mouth against hers.

There was a discreet knock on the door.

"Go away," he commanded.

"I do not wish to intrude, my lord." Westerby's voice was apologetic. "But Her Grace is asking for Miss Fairburn. It is, I believe, a question of the final arrangements for the arrival of Mrs. Fairburn and her family."

"Oh, heavens! So little time. Everything is going to be so complicated! Darcy, if someone is trying to kill Ceddie?"

"They won't succeed. Trust me." He kissed the top of her head. "Do you want me to speak to him about Melissa?"

She tried to assemble her thoughts. "No. I will suggest that we invite her over for tea, and you and I can tell them both together if that is agreeable to you?"

"As you will, my love."

He had called her his love. Her heart was beating so erratically she thought she would faint. But there was no time for that.

*   *   *

"Well, Grayson, someone is clearly bent on murder, and time is running out. Do you have any thoughts?"

Grayson scratched his head. "It's a re'glar mystery, my lord."

"Which it is fast becoming desperate that we solve. Someone wants my cousin, Cedric, dead. And, as I have already explained to you, to my knowledge there are only four people who would benefit from his death."

"Well, there's you out, for a start, m'lord."

Darcy inclined his head. "Thank you, Grayson. Your faith in me is touching. And his mother can be eliminated, for similar reasons. Which leaves my Uncle Eustace and my mama. Eustace is frequently in dun territory, but that is hardly an inducement to murder, and as for my mother, I am forced to confess she has an incredibly selfish streak, and money slips through her fingers like water. But she knows that, however much I complain, I will always frank her, should she arrive at *point non plus*. Besides which, at the moment, the viscount seems to be accomodating her very cordially."

Grayson coughed apologetically. "Forgive me, sir, but I think we should at least give some further thought to Sir Eustace. That was a bit of a havey-cavey business over Starlight. Never quite rang true, to my mind. An' nobody didn't never get to *examine* the damage to that ankle of his, if you take my meaning. Could have been meant to put us off the scent, give 'im an alibi, like. And there was that pretty boy as 'e was keepin' down the Dog and Partridge. He might well've left when 'is lordship did, but there's no saying but what he might 'ave come back somewhere's else."

"He didn't strike me as the violent type."

Grayson tipped his cap back and scratched his head.

"You can never tell with them pretty boys, m'lord. I've seen 'em turn quite vicious on occasion."

"You could be right." Darcy sighed. "To tell the truth, it's a disagreeable business all round when family's involved."

"Well, my money's on Sir Eustace, m'lord. Your ma may be selfish, but he has a downright ruthless way with him."

"Whoever it is, time is now desperately short. Muster as many men as you can, Grayson—men you can trust, and we'll mount a round-the-clock guard on my poor cousin. Thank God, he don't realize what's going on."

Cedric was surprised and not altogether helpful when Serena suggested driving over to invite Melissa to tea.

"You have kept promising to show her your butterfly collection and your paintings, Ceddie, but if you don't do it soon, we shall be much too busy."

"I doubt she'll want to come at such short notice."

"Nonsense. Melissa always enjoys coming to Masham." She gave him a sidelong glance. "I think perhaps she is a trifle lonely, with only her father and her old nurse for company."

Serena was at her most persuasive. A morning going through arrangements with the duchess had only reinforced the complexity of the situation. She had been left feeling deceitful and decidedly uncomfortable. The sooner the matter was resolved, the better.

Even so, it was a reluctant and silent Cedric who sat beside her in the phaeton on the way to Sir Lionel's house after luncheon. Melissa was surprised to see them, blushed, and made any number of excuses, all of which Serena overruled.

"Of course you must go, my love," Sir Lionel said, coming in on the end of the conversation. "It will do you good. You haven't been out of the house for days. Can't have you looking peaky for the wedding, what?"

It was not the most persuasive of arguments, but Melissa could hardly refuse without arousing his curiosity. They drove back in silence, Melissa being careful not to sit next to Cedric, though she longed to do so.

The arrangement had been that she and Darcy should tell them when they were all together in the studio. But suddenly, Serena looking from one wretched face to the other, could remain silent no longer.

"Pull up, Ceddie," she said in a voice that made him stare.

"Whatever for? Are you unwell?"

"No. At least . . . just do as I ask, dear boy."

She wondered how to begin, and then decided that the plain straightforward truth was the best.

"My dear, dear friends, I had meant to wait until we were back at Masham, but I cannot stand this air of gloom one moment longer."

They both looked mystified.

"Ceddie," she said, "I have to tell you that, fond as I am of you, I cannot marry you."

They both stared, momentarily deprived of speech.

"But Serena, you can't . . . all is arranged . . ."

"I must. You see, the truth is, I have fallen deeply in love with Darcy, and he with me."

Melissa uttered a tiny shriek, while Cedric looked at her suspiciously. "You can't have done. You are forever quarrleling."

"I know. That is sometimes the way with two strong-minded people, I believe. We shall probably continue so to do. But there it is. We cannot live without one another." Serena saw the dawning of hope in Melissa's face. "And as

anyone with half an eye can see that the two of you are eating your hearts out for each other, we decided that something should be done about it before it is too late."

Cedric still stared at her suspiciously. "You aren't just
being kind . . ."

She laughed. "Only to ourselves. Oh, Ceddie, have you
ever known Darcy do anything so unselfish?"

It was not their idea of a loverlike remark, which was
what finally convinced Cedric that it wasn't just a hum.

"So we hatched a little plan," Serena continued, "that
you should invite Melissa to see your collection and your
paintings, and we could all talk over what must be done
about it—and how best to break the news to your mama."

He continued to look at her, but believing now. "Serena,
I don't know what to say. She will be furious."

"At first, yes. But we'll talk her round."

As they drove up to the front entrance of Masham, it was
beginning to mist, and the sky was heavy with rain or
snow. A groom waited at the front steps to take the carriage
to the stables, and Cedric ushered the two ladies inside.
Their coats removed, the three prepared to make their way
down the corridor leading to Cedric's suite and his studio.

"Is Lord Lynton not here, Westerby?" Serena hung back
to ask.

"I have not seen him since this morning, Miss Fairburn,"
the butler replied.

"Well, when he comes, will you tell him where we are."

She hurried after the young couple, and as they turned at
the end of the corridor, they saw Mr. Bickerstaffe running
toward them in a state of great agitation.

"Oh, Your Grace, thank God that you are come! The
most terrible thing—your studio is ablaze! I was on my
way to summon help!"

"Where is Grove?"

"I don't know, sir—there was no sign of him. I had just come in by the side door and smelled smoke, and when I looked—well, I thought I had better get help."

Serena thought he had far better go to the stables and said so.

Cedric was already beginning to run. "Yes, Bickerstaffe, go quickly to the stables. They can use water from the pump there . . . I must see what can be saved!"

"Come back, Ceddie," Serena called to him. "You must not venture too close . . . the smoke will get on your chest!"

"Oh, do come back, Ceddie!" Melissa cried, though it was doubtful if he heard. So they both ran after him.

At first glance the fire didn't seem too bad. A log had fallen from the grate and rolled onto some papers stacked on the floor. These in turn had caught light and begun to float, setting fire to a half-finished painting on the center table.

"Oh, Ceddie, your work!"

"Never mind that. My butterfly collection is in the cupboard. If we can save that . . ." He opened the cupboard door and began to take out the boxes. Melissa ran to help.

"Put them outside in the corridor for now, well away from harm." The smoke was already making him cough.

"Ceddie, I can do that," Serena pleaded. "You mustn'· stay in here!"

But Melissa was back, her face ashen, her eyes wide with fear. "I can't open the door. It's locked and there is no key."

"It can't be locked!" Cedric tried it, then stumbled across to the other door leading to the terrace. That, too, was locked. He turned, leaning against it, gasping for breath. "Someone has . . . we're trapped!"

Serena's fear was channeled by sheer desperation into seeking a way to survive until help came, as come it must.

The threat to Cedric's life had now assumed a terrifying reality, and unless she could think of something, she and Melissa would die with him.

The windows offered no means of escape. They were composed entirely of small panes, several of which were already cracking with the heat. Soon they would let in air to feed the flames. She pushed the boxes back into the cupboard and slammed the door shut, then ran across to the small stone sink, where two bowls of water were always kept so that Cedric would wash his brushes.

"Melissa, take off your petticoat quickly and bring it here!"

She was already loosing the strings of her own. Melissa hesitated for no more than a second or two.

Cedric was already beginning to gasp painfully as she dunked the petticoats in the water, lifted them, and wrung them out. Oh, Darcy, where are you? she cried silently.

"Help him over here, Melissa . . . the smoke is less thick. Ceddie, crouch down and put one of these right over you, like a tent. You, too, Melissa. Don't argue . . . just do it. There's a towel here I can use . . . " The smoke was beginning to choke her. "It will . . . keep the worst away for a while . . . and someone must come soon . . ."

The second bucket of water she flung recklessly across the area where they were, and also around the cupboard. Then she squatted down with the other two and waited. And prayed as she had never prayed before.

Lady Charlotte and the viscount were on the point of leaving Masham for a drive as Darcy rode in that afternoon.

"Don't wish to be a killjoy, Lynton, but that smoke back there wouldn't be coming from His Grace's stables, would it?"

Darcy saw the thin black spiral and his immediate thought was for the horses.

"I'll set Charlotte down and follow you," the viscount called after him as Darcy drove his horse at a gallop, holding it on course as it tried to jig away with fear, the smoke already in its nostrils.

He found the stable lads already making a chain of buckets from the pump in the yard. But the fire was coming from just beyond the trees. Cedric's quarters. Surely it couldn't be . . . He slid from the saddle and ran.

"Hurly! What the devil?"

"His Grace's rooms. Thank God someone noticed it. We're moving as fast as we can, but it's already taken hold."

"Is His Grace inside?"

"We don't know, m'lord."

Darcy thought of the projected tea party. Serena! All three of them. Dear God! He waited to hear no more, but ran, stumbling over the ground until he reached the studio, where flames were licking the edges of the windows and smoke curled out from splintering glass.

"Is anyone inside?" he shouted again.

"No sign of life near the windows, m'lord."

He ran on. The door was fast. "Someone lend me a strong shoulder!"

One of the grooms ran across and together they made a concerted assault on the door.

"It's no use. We need to force the lock!"

The man fished in his big pouch pocket and brought out an iron hoof pick. Within moments, though it seemed like hours, there was a click, the door opened, and heat and smoke rushed out.

Darcy ducked his head and ran in. "Serena? Cedric? Is there anyone here? For God's sake, answer!"

From almost under his feet, the thread of a beloved voice wheezed, "Darcy!" The smoke stung his eyes, but he could see what looked like three sacks. "Take Cedric first . . ." Serena whispered. "We can manage . . ."

Once they were out of the studio, Cedric and Melissa were taken into the house, but Serena could not bear to be indoors. She needed to breathe some fresh air in her lungs, so Darcy had thrown his cloak round her and left her sitting on a tree stump. Lady Charlotte came to keep her company and was surprisingly kind.

The stables had been more or less neglected while everyone who had been busy fighting the fire stood around collecting their breath and their wits, so that no one at first noticed the man who crept out of a far stall, leading one of the horses. He tried to mount up, but the smell of fire had caught in the animal's nostrils, and it backed and reared, whinnying nervously.

"I knows that cove!" Jack cried in ringing accents that brought Darcy to the scene. "An' I know where I seen 'im, an' all, Guv! It was in the Crossed Keys that time Trumpeter cast a shoe and we 'ad to put up fer the night, an' Miss Fairburn wus set on when she wus asleep! I remember, cos he wus arskin' a lot of questions . . ." Jack's voice took on a note of urgency. "Look out, Guv—'e knows 'e's been rumbled—'e's lopin' off!"

"It's Julian!" Lady Charlotte cried faintly. "Oh, do have a care, Darcy, there must be some mistake!"

"Bickerstaffe!"

Darcy was upon him before he had gone more than a yard or two. And there was no mistaking his guilt, for it was mingled with fury in the twisted face. A red mist swam before Darcy's eyes, and it took the viscount and Grayson to pull him away, while a couple of the grooms wrestled him to the ground.

"Oh, Julian! The fire . . . how could you!" Lady Charlotte sobbed.

As they hauled Mr. Bickerstaffe upright, he leaned forward, his face red and distorted.

"Bitch!" he screamed. "It was for you! I did it for you—for us! You told me that you only suffered that common creature Morville for his money, and how it was my company that made his presence bearable. You begged me to be patient . . . that soon you expected to inherit, then everything would be different! I know all about poverty—the scrimping and scraping, the way people you had supposed to be your friends cut you dead . . . "

"So, you thought you would kill my cousin, and recoup your position." Darcy ground the words out.

"She used to talk to me about you all—about the duke's failing health . . . and how you'd all be rich when he died! You should have heard how she carried on when she learned he was getting married . . . as good as inciting me to do something about it!"

"No! Oh, no, never that!" Charlotte was moaning, though nobody heeded her. They were all riveted to the words that were pouring out of the deranged man as he turned on her once more.

"I as good as told you I would find a way! B-but you couldn't wait, could you, greedy bitch! *He* came along—" Bickerstaffe stabbed a finger at the viscount and stared round at them all, wild-eyed. "I had to do what I did, don't you see? It was my only hope . . ." He began to cry.

"Oh, no! You are quite wrong! I have never . . . would never . . . it is quite horrible!" whispered Lady Charlotte, clutching at Serena's arm. Then she fainted away.

The duchess suddenly looked ten years older, Serena thought, watching the older woman. Her bombastic air of

authority had deserted her, leaving her a rather pathetic figure hunched in her chair.

It was several hours now since the fire had been extinguished, and much had happened—too much for her to take
in. She had finally been banished by the doctor from the
room where her son was fighting for his life, and ordered to
rest, but she refused to go and lie down for fear that Cedric
would die while she slept. Melissa, though in no danger,
had been given a draught, and was asleep in one of the
guest rooms, her father at her side.

Serena could not rest, however. She had refused to take
any physic, though her chest still ached, and she thought
she would never rid herself of the smell of smoke. The
events of those terrible hours were still seared into her
mind.

"Is there anything I can do for you, ma'am?" she asked,
laying a hand on the duchess's arm.

A veined hand covered hers. "Thank you, child, I believe
I have not always valued you as I ought"—the words came
painfully slowly—"but never think I am not aware that if
my poor son lives, it will be due to your presence of mind.
Now, all we can do is wait."

"Cedric is holding his own, you know," Serena said encouragingly. "In fact, Dr. Handley thinks he stands a very
good chance of recovering."

There was no immediate reply, and Serena was left to reflect on all that had happened.

Melissa had sustained no lasting injuries, but Grove,
poor Grove, had been found unconscious with a head
wound and had not yet recovered consciousness. The viscount had left shortly after the constable had come to remove Mr. Bickerstaffe, and Lady Charlotte had retired to
her bed in a distressed state, uncertain whether the viscount
would ever wish to see her again. Serena believed that this

time her affections were truly engaged and could not help feeling sorry for her.

"I have written to put my family off coming, for the present, at least."

"How thoughtful. You were looking forward to seeing them, I know. But it will be for the best." The duchess's voice trembled. "Until we know."

"Honestly, I would rather have her looking down that autocratic nose and barking orders at me," Serena said later as she nestled in the curve of Darcy's arm.

They were alone in the Yellow Saloon, and everywhere was quiet. The candlelight was restful, and for a while she had almost forgotten her various aches and pains.

"She's a tough old bird. She'll come about presently, you'll see. So make the most of your freedom while you can."

He looked down at her, his expression inscrutable, though his voice was not quite steady. "I suppose you realize that you robbed me of ten years of my life today. When I saw the state you were in . . ." His voice hardened. "I wanted to kill that man with my bare hands."

"What he did was very dreadful, of course," Serena mused. "But I believe his misfortune turned his mind, so in a way one can understand his bitterness."

"You may. I would just like to wring his neck very slowly."

"Perhaps. But, in fairness, your mother did encourage his expectations. I saw them together, heard her . . ."

He looked at her sardonically. "You mean she flirted with him—toyed with his affections? Of course she did. She flirts with every man she meets. But only a fool or a knave would take her seriously."

"How shocking. Which is the viscount, I wonder?" she

mused. "You know, I really thought she might have met her match in him. Will he forgive her, do you think?"

"I devoutly hope so, my practical optimistic love, or I am like to become her banker again."

She nestled closer. "Am I? Your love, I mean?"

He demonstrated the fact to her entire satisfaction.

"I suppose we shall have to wait a while—see how long it takes Ceddie to recover before we can sort everything out."

"Not if I can help it," he retorted swiftly. "The dowager owes her son's life to you. And since she seems to be aware of that, I hope she may reward you accordingly."

"I am so glad Ceddie's butterfly collection was saved. But almost all his paintings were destroyed. It does seem so unfair."

"He will be able to paint them all again when he is well, and when he is not mooning over that silly child," said her beloved ruthlessly.

"Melissa is not silly. And she will be very good for him, I think. He will insist on looking after her instead of people forever looking after him."

"How very perceptive of you. Now that you have arranged everyone else's lives, I wonder if I might have your attention for a moment. I would like to talk about us."

"Yes, indeed my lord," Serena murmured meekly. "What aspect of 'us' would your lordship like to discuss?".

Chapter Eighteen

It was a day in early spring, with daffodils and hyacinths in bloom and the first blossom in bud when everyone gathered at Masham to see Miss Serena Fairburn married to Darcy, sixth Earl of Lynton.

The bride looked radiant in her simple pale gray gown with the jet beading, which had been made for quite a different occasion. Her shining chestnut hair was dressed high and crowned with a tiny cap made of pearls and jet beads.

His lordship cut an equally handsome figure in a coat of darker gray made for him by Weston, a handsome brocade waistcoat, a cravat of wonderful complexity, and black small clothes. For a man who had exercised more patience than was his wont, he looked remarkably sanguine.

The wedding had been delayed until Cedric was well enough to attend. His recovery had been slow, but Dr. Handly was of the opinion that he would suffer no lasting harm.

The bride was given in marriage by her eldest brother, a handsome figure in full dress uniform, who was sighed over by all the ladies. And Lady Charlotte was with her viscount, who had surprised himself and everyone else by forgiving her pecadilloes, and she resolved that in future nothing should be allowed to come between them. The viscount's friends were already taking bets as to how long it would be before he lost his bachelor status.

The Fairburn family were there in their entirety, with the children on their best behavior, watched over by Miss Abby.

It had come as something of a shock to Mrs. Fairburn to learn that her daughter's plans had been so abruptly changed. But the knowledge that the earl was almost as rich as Cedric, as well as being much more influential in social circles, soon had her singing his praises. And her first visit to Ashbourne House set the seal of approval on the union. It was, she declared, exactly the kind of country house one would wish for, pleasantly proportioned and nothing like so overwhelming as Masham.

Edward also approved his sister's change of heart. "I do like the duke very well," he'd said. "But he don't have a bang-up rig like the earl."

Mrs. Fairburn, as might be expected, cried throughout the ceremony, which incensed the Dowager Duchess of Cornwell.

"Silly woman!" she was heard to mutter. "The child's done remarkably well for herself. Almost as well as she might have done had she married my son."

And she had glanced proudly at Cedric, who sat next to her, now almost recovered from his dreadful experience of a few months back.

The duchess had not realized how much she had come to depend on Serena until it was too late. It was with very real regret that she sanctioned the end of the betrothal, but anyone with half an eye could see that Serena and Darcy were in love, and it was the least she could do. She had not at first considered Melissa Glenville old enough or mature enough to be given care of Cedric, but there was no doubting the girl's devotion to her son during his long, slow recovery.

It was Sir Lionel who had talked her round. And, to be sure, Melissa had a very natural sweetness of disposition and was very willing to listen to advice.

It had been decided that the need to rush into marriage was not paramount, and that Melissa would therefore make her debut in London society before her marriage. The duchess had been less keen to agree that Cedric, if well enough, should visit London for a short time, but dear Serena's offer to allow him to stay with them persuaded her.

Serena would be in London to attend to Emily's comeout at the same time—a beautiful child with a face like an angel. Empty-headed, of course, but with such looks she would doubtless be married within the twelvemonth. Her Grace was still not entirely happy to let Cedric out of her sight for even a short time, but Serena had given assurance that he would be most carefully looked after, and Grove, now almost fit to resume his duties, would go with him.

At the reception in the blue drawing room later, Serena made her way across the room to Cedric. He held out his hands to her, his gentle smile very evident as he reached out to kiss her cheek.

"I owe you so much, dear Cousin," he said, "that I scarcely know where to begin. My life, for a start. Without you, I should not be here now."

"Please. Let us not think of that now. This is a day for celebration, and we are very much in each other's debt," she returned affectionately. "But for you, I would not have met Darcy."

She could scarcely believe he had made such a full recovery. That dreadful day was now little more than a bad dream.

"Unhand my wife, sirrah," said Darcy, coming up behind them. He lifted a sardonic eyebrow. "I suppose one must go through all this nonsense, but for my part"—he looked at Serena in a way that made her blush—"it cannot end soon enough."

And end it did, with Serena in a deep purple velvet traveling gown and a high-crowned matching bonnet adorned with feathers, taking leave of all her family. Her mama cried again, which surprised no one.

"Be happy, my dear! So fortunate . . . I declare that his lordship is every bit as handsome as your dear papa . . ." Here her words became tearful and indistinct.

"She will be all right, directly," said Abby, giving Serena a hug.

"Away with you," said the duchess. "If you don't go soon, your mama will become a regular watering pot."

Serena kissed her cheek, and though Her Grace professed to dislike such demonstrations, Serena thought she was not displeased.

"Enough," said Darcy and removed her almost forcibly.

On the forecourt a splendid carriage with a liveried coachman up on the box awaited them. As did Edward, who was being given instructions by Jack on how to control a high-couraged pair of horses.

"Na. Not like that, young sprig! Yer got ter let 'em know yer the boss, but gentlelike! Not cow-handed!"

"I believe this is almost where we came in," said the earl, handing his wife up into the carriage. "Let them go, Jack," he commanded.

As the carriage bowled down the drive amid the cheers of the guests and servants, his lordship could be clearly seen removing his wife's beautiful feathered hat. Thereafter, both parties disappeared from view.